THE WORK OF
Saint
Francis

MacKINLAY KANTOR

Rain and
the Feast of the
Stars

Reiko Hatsumi

THE WORK OF SAINT FRANCIS

THE WORK OF
Saint Francis

BY

MacKINLAY KANTOR

ILLUSTRATIONS BY JOHANNES TROYER

THE WORLD PUBLISHING COMPANY

CLEVELAND AND NEW YORK

PUBLISHED BY The World Publishing Company
2231 West 110th Street, Cleveland 2, Ohio

PUBLISHED SIMULTANEOUSLY IN CANADA BY
Nelson, Foster & Scott Ltd.

Library of Congress Catalog Card Number: 58-9411

FIRST EDITION

A shorter version, under the title "The Unseen
Witness," appeared in *The Saturday Evening Post*,
copyright 1954 by The Curtis Publishing Company.

WP758

BOOKS BY MacKINLAY KANTOR

Fiction

DIVERSEY • EL GOES SOUTH • THE JAYBIRD

LONG REMEMBER • THE VOICE OF BUGLE ANN

AROUSE AND BEWARE • THE ROMANCE OF ROSY RIDGE

THE NOISE OF THEIR WINGS • HERE LIES HOLLY SPRINGS

VALEDICTORY • CUBA LIBRE • GENTLE ANNIE

HAPPY LAND • AUTHOR'S CHOICE • GLORY FOR ME

MIDNIGHT LACE • WICKED WATER • THE GOOD FAMILY

ONE WILD OAT • SIGNAL THIRTY-TWO • DON'T TOUCH ME

WARWHOOP • THE DAUGHTER OF BUGLE ANN

GOD AND MY COUNTRY • ANDERSONVILLE

Juvenile

ANGLEWORMS ON TOAST

LEE AND GRANT AT APPOMATTOX

GETTYSBURG

Personalia

BUT LOOK, THE MORN

LOBO

Verse

TURKEY IN THE STRAW

ABOUT THE AUTHOR

MacKinlay Kantor was born in Webster City, Iowa, February 4, 1904. He started to write seriously at the age of sixteen, and his first novel was published in 1928. Since then thirty-two of his books have been appreciated by readers in America and abroad: verse, collections of short stories and novelettes, juvenile books, histories, and many novels, with a crowning achievement in the latter field—the monumental *Andersonville*, for which the author was awarded the Pulitzer Prize. MacKinlay Kantor's accomplishments include one of the most famous motion pictures of all time, *The Best Years of Our Lives*, for which he wrote the original story. By no means solely devoted to the art of authorship, Mr. Kantor has achieved combat experience in two wars, and was personally decorated by the commander of the United States Air Force.

Mr. Kantor is married to Irene Layne, the artist. They are the parents of Layne Shroder, who in 1957 published her first novel. Their son, Tim Kantor, is a professional photographer and a former Air Force flyer.

The home of the Kantors is at Sarasota, Florida, although in recent years they have lived often abroad, especially in Spain, where Mr. Kantor wrote most of *Andersonville* and absorbed the background for this book.

To
Ruth Dowdell

THE WORK OF SAINT FRANCIS

BROTHER ANDRÉS was on night duty, checking the cells. Blanco knew the step of each preceptor, as most of the ninety-odd other boys in the reformatory knew their steps. Brother Andrés walked forever with nervous haste.

Flat and naked on his bed, Blanco waited without drawing a breath.

Next door to the left, now, the friar was opening the cell where El Pecas slept: a plump boy of twelve, his face smeared with orange and brown freckles like scars or burns. Blanco loved El Pecas, and a wetness started beneath his squeezed eyelids as he realized that in the morning he would be gone, he would never see his chum again.

Keys, the rattle of chain and keys, the swish of Brother Andrés' robes. *How do I look when I'm truly asleep?* was the thought which worried Blanco. *Like this? Or—* He managed to unclench one fist; he must appear to be at peace, dead to the small tight world of the institution, dead to the ominous black world of Spanish mountain slopes outside.

The wooden door swung with the usual keen squeaking of its upper hinge; now the boy knew that he was spread innocently to the friar's gaze. He was breathing again, trying to breathe regularly, the stupid soft

breathing of an inert sleeper. No matter that
his eyes were pressed shut, his head turned
aside: he saw Brother Andrés clearly with
the practiced lens of experience and imagi-
nation . . . standing thin and solemn and
round-shouldered, his head on one side as
he peered, his sparse beard a tangle against
the lighted courtyard.

Door squeak, key wrenching in the lock,
jingle and jangle, scurry of woolen habit,
the hasty step receding. There was one more
cell just beyond, but it lay vacant. A tall
youth named Juan Bedia had dwelt there,
a refugee from the older boys' dormitory
which was full to overflowing. Juan had
snored beyond the high partition at Blanco's
right hand; but advancing age freed him—
if you could call the Army freedom. Older
boys went into the Army at twenty-one
unless their sentences expired earlier; then

they went home until the Army claimed them.

The sentence of Ambrosio Blanco Sanz y Merida would expire in another two months, but he knew what would happen then; it had been demonstrated in the case of other *prisioneros*. Blanco was an orphan; his mother had died during the first month of his sentence. As an orphan he would continue to dwell in the *reformatorio*—perhaps through seven years until the time of his military service.

Brother Andrés locked the outer door of the cell room, and his pace and rustle could be heard no longer. Blanco bounced up into dense darkness as if hurled by a spring. In his mind he had practiced every gesture a hundred times since the notion of escape began to gnaw him. Here was his faded blue shirt, here were his ragged shorts; the *al-*

pargatas lay neatly side by side beneath the chair, and his fingers trembled only slightly as he tied them on.

(If he became a successful smuggler, he would wear shoes of shiny leather—not straw sandals which he had helped to make, and all the other boys had helped to make, there in the sandal shop at that school. He would sit each evening in front of a café on the coastal highway, a glass of *anís* beside him. And when a poor bootblack arose from shining his shoes, Blanco would give him not one but two pesetas. On his birthday, or on his saint's day, he might toss to the *limpiabotas* as much as five pesetas, and be blessed for it.)

On a cord around his neck he wore a religious medal which Brother Marco had given him when Blanco lay in the grip of pneumonia the previous winter. Truly he had been very sick—close to death—though Blanco could remember little about it except ache and stifling and frightening pictures dancing like a fast-thumbed comic book through his brain. The other monks said that it was Brother Marco's nursing which had saved the boy; but fervently Brother Marco attributed the recovery to that same medal, and to Saint Francis himself.

The medal, his rosary, and his towel. Blanco had no other personal possession in the world. Once he had owned a pocket-knife with one broken blade, and a red plastic cigarette holder. Both of these wealths he had found by the roadside when the boys were being marched to the beach in summertime. But the treasures had been discovered and taken from him—the one on practical, the other on ethical grounds.

. . . Oh, also a handkerchief; it was red

and white, it romped across the playground in a high wind. He had adored that hand-kerchief, but a bigger boy stole it. Blanco was certain that the boy had it, but he kept it secreted somewhere or other, and lied in-dignantly when the Brothers questioned him. They did not whip Alonso; they thought Blanco must be mistaken. . . .

Now he feared, he feared many things. He feared the heavy strap of Brother Marco, waiting for him the next day. He feared the golden German shepherd bitch in the patio below, and most of all he feared the Civil Guards patrolling the highway. But his ambition rose above these terrors, and in braving the menace of the dog and the Guards he would at least leave the threat of the strap behind him.

(If he became a rich *contrabandista*—there were many in Spain—he might purchase an

automobile. Or at least a motorcycle . . .
yes, a motorcycle of gleaming silver and
blue. He would come bouncing across the
uneven ground before the reformatory door,
his engine popping like machine-gun fire . . .
"*Chiquito!* Yes, I mean you—boy beside the
door. Go and tell Brother Marco that an
old friend has called to see him . . . Aha,
Brother Marco, little did you think to see
me with this motorcycle! What about those
blows of the belt you promised, so long ago?
Do you wish to proceed with my punishment now? Aha-aha! Well then, here—I have
a little gift for you—for you and the reformatory, and for all *los niños pobres*. Accept it with my affection. A thousand-peseta
note. Surely you do not object to a gift of
one thousand pesetas? Come, come, take it
—I have many more!")

He feared—

The partition rose round his cubicle to a height that had seemed enormous when he was smaller. As Blanco stood balancing silently on the footrail of his metal cot, he could hold his desperate left hand upstretched and see the blackness ending sharply and the grayness beginning sharply, perhaps a meter beyond his fingers. He would have to jump with the skill of a monkey to clamp his grasp on the top of that partition.

For a long time he had practiced. He was left-handed, his left arm was stronger than his right. He dared not practice in his cell when other boys were about, and only on the rarest of occasions had he ever stood alone in that dormitory.

But there was a truncated acacia tree on the edge of the playground, and one limb jutted out at a height comparable with the height of the cell partition when Blanco was

standing on the bed's frame. Slyly he measured the acacia limb with a stick, and he
measured that stick against himself, and later
measured himself against the chair in his cell.
The identical height—in fact the acacia limb
was very slightly higher.

Then, if he could learn to crouch and
leap straight into the air beneath the acacia
limb, and snatch deftly at the branch and
swing himself up and over it, he was con-
fident that he could attain the partition's top,
and so leave his cell forever.

Never afterward did he pass beneath that
tree, at work or in play, without springing
at the branch. Soon he was able to seize it,
but only by taking a running jump. A standing jump was much more difficult; he needed
to grow taller, to have longer legs and arms.
. . . He had them at last, now that he was
nearly fourteen. For three weeks he had

been able to grasp the acacia almost at will; he'd missed only twice; he must not miss the partition now.

If he did miss, he would crash down upon his bed and probably go through the frail flat spring. Thus other boys would be aroused, and so would the Capuchinos downstairs or in rooms beyond; and so the strap, and so no more nourishing soup or rich *cocido*— nothing but bread and water for a week at least; and allowed to speak to no one, or to be spoken to.

He must not miss.

READY for departure, the corded soles of his sandals bent across the metal rail, the muscles of his skinny legs tensing. Blanco bit at his lower lip until the salt of blood came . . . he strove for air, he could find no air, barely did he hold a scream in check. Every string of his frame seemed stretched upward, upward. He was an arrow, a bullet; and also he was the weapon—machine and projectile, all in one.

He flew suspended while whole seconds went ticking away. Blanco thought of the big clock in the Reverend Father's office . . . *tawk, tawk, tawk* . . . something pained and scraped his hand. The partition's top. He had reached it, he had claimed it, it was claiming him.

Writhing and twisting, he forced his right arm aloft; the fingers slipped, touched, slipped again . . . there, *there*. Both hands gripping. His body was pliant and agile, it curved like a snake. One bare ankle dragged across, the bare leg wiggled after it; in another moment Blanco sat sobbing and sweaty, astride the partition. He had made much more noise than he'd intended. He listened with his two ears—it seemed that he had a dozen ears, all reaching out for accusing sounds.

Nada. Nothing, nothing, nothing. Limón was coughing in his sleep, which was an ordinary occurrence; and little Angel was having a nightmare, and wailing about it, and mumbling rapidly, "Mother, mother, mother," and this also was an ordinary occurrence.

Blanco hitched his way to the front wall of the cubicle, hung on the outer side, and dropped. Perhaps this was as dangerous a moment as any other. It sounded like thunder when he struck the hall floor, corded straw soles or no corded straw soles. He crouched, listening again. *Nada.* Well, often one of the boys fell out of his narrow bed at night; and, too, the carpentry shop was directly beneath, and it was unlikely that anyone would be in the carpentry shop after midnight.

Opening opposite locked doors of the nine cubicles in that row, wide windows offered their glory of cool night air, the air of freedom. Outside the windows lay a sloping roof of tile, supported by stone columns.

Blanco Sanz was a hasty shadow, catfooted across the rosy tiles. He felt the crush of morning-glory vines beneath his sandals . . . oh, beauty. Those velvet flowers with their luscious borders of purple-blue, their centers of pink: they looked good enough to eat when the sun widened and warmed them. Actually Blanco had tried to eat them a time or two . . . never had he walked on the vines before.

Tendrils wound his ankles; he came close to pitching to death on the patio floor, but he recovered his balance and soon lay safely at the farthest, lowest corner of the roof. Rooting his hands deep among the vines he found a gnarled rope of grape bark which weighted underneath. He had tested that vine in full view of the monks, and it seemed they had never dreamed what was in his mind. The thick strand of grape would support his body, it did support his body. Down he went, and stood at last with scratches and throbbing heartbeats alone in the court.

No, not alone. She came toward him steadily, moving her great paws in deliberate pace. Regina, the shepherd bitch, and what stories were told about her . . . a silent beast, unheeding the noisy throngs of boys tall and small who trooped past her every hour. She might lie motionless through a whole morning work session or class session, her rubber nose on her paws, her yellow eyes dreaming; yet older prisoners in the crew never tired of frightening the little folks, the nine- and ten-year-olds, with tales of Regina's murderous prowess.

Boys who were trying to escape: they said that Regina had a knack with them. She could spring like the great pale wolf she was, her jaws sure and avenging. Even the blow of a heavy club would glance harmlessly off her thick body. Who was that burly youth—did they call him El Rubio?— And he was imprisoned for knifing a night watchman at the nearby country club. He had tried to batter his way to independence, striking at the dog with an iron pipe, but she had nearly pulled the arm off him. At least, so the legend went.

One *garbanzo*, saved carefully by Blanco each day. He deplored giving up that single greasy chick-pea . . . rations were small, even the friars' rations were meager; they had to be, on an official allowance of five pesetas per boy per day. Still he always saved a *garbanzo* for Regina, and other people thought that he was crazy to do it.

He would offer the sullen dog the rich

pea—bigger than his thumbnail, often. He would say softly, *"Perrita,"* and the first time he did this she showed her teeth, so in fear and trembling he tossed the gift to the ground. But she ate it later, he saw her eat it; and the next time she did not snarl—she only looked at him squarely. For several weeks he had fed her those bits, speaking in affection each time; at last she would take them from his fingers.

But he feared her.

She was a fluffy hulk beside him, and actually her damp hard nose pushed his leg.

"Perrita," he whispered. Oh, where was that scrap of bone he had saved from his last meal? There had been goat meat in the evening stew, and a minor portion of the meat had come Blanco's way. He had consumed it fiercely, but he'd saved the broken chunk of bone.

Not in this pocket, not— And the enormous dog frozen beside him. . . . Here, here! In his hip pocket, underneath the towel which he had wadded. Regina accepted the fragment and, never stirring in her tracks, began to crush the bone.

A door opened suddenly at the end of the patio. Blanco sank back against the cushioned morning-glories. Brother Andrés was bustling directly toward him, and the mutter of his prayer came ahead. Unless stricken suddenly blind, how could the monk fail to see Blanco, and haul him to justice?

On, on he came, chanting softly; it was a habit of Brother Andrés to offer prayers as he worked and walked; only in the dormitories did he keep a silence at night, fearing to waken the tired boys.

He did not see Blanco at all. Perhaps shadows had tricked him, for there was one electric lamp burning at this end of the court, and a lopsided moon now rose out of the Mediterranean. A cry choked in the throat of Blanco—he fought it, deadened it—he felt a warm spurt of water on his leg. Then the man had said politely, "Good night, Regina," and had gone scooting past. Brother Andrés opened the door of the chapel hall in the rear building, he vanished, and the door was closed, and there was no sound except the grating noise made by Regina with her bone.

A few seconds later Blanco was in the darkened smithy which formed the west wall of the reformatory, picking his way among grates and grilles. The shrunken moon helped him even in its distant reflection.

This window, the one directly behind the anvil. Once there had been glass in all the frames, but accidents had accounted for most of the panes, despite heavy guarding screens.

These Capuchinos did not believe in bars. They desired to teach and restrain the boys, but felt that bars would be a constant, insurmountable reminder of their plight. "Regina is enough, in herself," Brother Marco had said. "And the fact that the boys are locked up for the night. Very few runaways do we have."

Certainly he reckoned without Blanco. The boy bent the loose steel screen and went through the window feet first. He dropped to the ground and kept close to the blot of buildings until he had reached the front. There was a wall beside the road but the gate stood open carelessly, night and day.

No Civil Guards walked their endless beats; seldom did they patrol that cart-path. It was a narrow course, studded with rocks, difficult for cars or trucks to negotiate. Most

of the traffic consisted of carts and *mulos*
and black-clad women trudging on foot, and
none of these would be seen in the middle
of the night.

Blanco dashed across the road and down
the hillside path toward the sea. He knew
this route well; it was the way they walked
when the Brothers took them, in delighted
jabbering detachments, to swim in the sea.
Below that hill, parallel to the beach, stretched
the hard-paved length of the main coastal
highway. This highway led eventually to
Algeciras, and Algeciras was where the chief
smugglers were reputed to have their head-
quarters.

The fragment moon crawled from last
nets of clouds which lay across the sea, and
found the thin intent figure running there.

ONCE his father had been a trusted and respectable farmer, pruning the olives which belonged to Don Miguel Poveda, plowing with solemn black oxen on the hill beside a toppling Moorish tower. That was long ago—long before Blanco was born. The mother had been a pretty woman, but frail and sickly; no children had yet come to her.

Then, in 1936, a truck filled with *comunistas* drove into the whitewashed courtyard

33

of Don Miguel's country house. They were yelling at the top of their lungs—some were drunk, some were not, some wore uniforms —and already they had five battered prisoners tied together in the truck. José Sanz came running from his cottage at hearing this uproar; he saw the communists dragging out Don Miguel and his crippled son, Don Angel. José had a hammer in his hand—he had been repairing a trellis. He fought hard.

"So you fight on the side of the aristocracy, the rich who have robbed and starved us?" they said, when they had overpowered him. "Very well—you shall get the same dose we give to them." José was carried off in the truck with the others, and men kicked his head all the way down to the dry creek valley, and thus he was unconscious when they dumped the prisoners off the old stone bridge. Pistols banged—the screaming women at the *finca* could hear them—and stolen shotguns too, and one machine gun.

All were dead except José Sanz. Don Miguel's riddled body was lying across José when relatives crept out to find them; it was as if the brave Don Miguel had tried to shield his servant. José would lurch and stagger through the rest of his days, because of those wounds in his legs which never healed. A friendly butcher from the town of Megalite amputated his arm and did a very good job—it was praised later by an Army doctor.

Blanco was not born until after the war ended, but he had known nothing but the poverty engendered by war. The Poveda family were all slain or scattered; thus Blanco was born in that same once-happy cottage, but there were no oxen or *mulos* any more, and the pretty *finca* had been looted and burnt out. It was hard for a lame one-armed man and a coughing woman to scratch a living from the soil, even when the disordered state of property titles permitted them to try it.

Then, when Blanco was five, a new owner appeared; he was some distant relative of the Povedas, and said that he had inherited the farm. He was a fat-faced fellow who sat in a little black *coche* and talked in short, unpleasant sentences. Unfortunate, he said. He had his own farmer, a man from Fuengirola. He would be arriving the next week, bringing livestock. He would need that cottage to live in while he plowed. It was January; time for plowing; look at the almond blossoms—already they were pink. . . .

The Sanz family went away, pushing their belongings in a handcart as if they were gypsies. Small as he was, Blanco could remember helping to push that cart on the steeper hills. They reached the sea on the second day and squatted in a stone shed at the edge of a fishing village.

José found part-time employment, helping with nets and boats, though he was too mutilated to be of value in the vessels when they sailed. He begged and borrowed seed, and all three worked long hours, carrying water from afar, tending their vines of tomatoes and melons. When these were ripe, Blanco and his mother would walk with baskets on their heads to Megalite, four *kilómetros* away, and sit offering fruit in the market. For early fruit they might receive as much as two pesetas a kilogram; later the price was apt to drop sharply.

Usually there were fish to put in the kettle; not, however, in bad weather. When storms blew unceasingly from the east for days on end, as was apt to happen in February and March, no boats could go out. Even children of the more prosperous fishermen—men who actually owned their own boats—even these children had often to stand begging outside the rich tourist hotels above the Megalite cliffs. Blanco learned to beg, but it enraged him to be mistaken for a gypsy, and thus he was apt to spit at the *turistas*, and that was no way to get pesetas out of anyone.

The old leg wounds pained José Sanz, and made it increasingly difficult for him to haul at the wet nets on the beach. If he had lived—say, in Málaga—he might have obtained a respectable post as guard in a parking area; all these jobs were given to wounded ex-soldiers, and surely some friends of the late Don Miguel would have helped José; he was a *mutilado* just as certainly as if he had

worn a uniform. But José had never lived
in a city in his life, and his wife and son
had never even seen a city. Where could
they find quarters to live in, in Málaga?

When Blanco was nearly eleven, a rich
man from Granada came to the seaside and
declared his intention of building a tourist
court and night club, right on the edge of
those sands. A side road would be cut, down
from the coastal highway; Señor Rata bought
up every square meter of land at the end
of that cluster of huts. He bought the very
land out from under the feet of the Sanz
family. His road would pass through the
stone shed where they had been squatters
for more than five years.

They stayed until men came with dynamite to blow up the shed. From the highway they looked back and saw the puffs
of dun smoke, the flying debris; they heard

39

the *boom*. They went on to curling brown cliffs east of Megalite, where there were several ancient caves. Shaggy, leering gypsies peered from three of the cluttered entrances, but the farthest cave was vacant except for a few goats, and Blanco drove these out with stones and shrieks. The Sanz family made a great weed bed, and huddled through the night without a fire; it had been too dark for them to find firewood, after they'd gathered the weeds.

Next day, José had a fever and his left leg was swollen and red; sometimes he slept heavily, and cried out in his sleep. Blanco caught some crabs, but José refused to eat. He said that he was worthless, and only a burden to those he loved; and now he wished that God would take him, and perhaps he would see once more his admired friend Don Miguel Poveda. . . . That night Blanco stole a kid while the goatherd was asleep, and at dawn he butchered it crudely on rocks where rising waves washed away the traces. His mother made a fine stew of the kid, but still José would not eat. He died before the week ended.

. . . How he managed to crawl that distance could not be imagined. José went out of the cave at some blackest hour of night, so quietly that neither Blanco nor María stirred. (It would have been a hideous thing, had he died in the cave. Who would have carried him away?— Could a narrow coffin, even a hundred-peseta coffin with a black tin cross tacked on the top?— Could it have been achieved? How? So there would be no slow march of the fishing-village men, carrying José upon their shoulders.)

Ever since he could remember, Blanco had lived among clay and stones—very close to clay and stones. Almost he was made of clay and stone himself: he had hair the color of limestone, his small blank hard eyes were the color of an eroded Malaguanan hillside, sun-parched, red-brown. With this affinity for the earth where he lived, it was easy for him to follow his father's slow-dragged route across that earth.

Out and far and far, up amid cactus and close-cut stumps of century plants, onto the narrow path where occasional tourists rambled to have a peek at the caves or to marvel at talkative shreds of the Mediterranean, plowing and speaking and folding insistently across polished slabs of dark rock some twenty meters below. . . .

Nearly as blue as morning-glory fabric, those waves in a bright daytime. They would have been black at night.

. . . And along that light-trodden footpath, and on to where the path faded among disordered boulders, and pebbles dripped into space. That was the way José had traveled, and if the nasty squealing little gypsy dogs had barked at him no one ever heard.

The sobbing María clutched her rosary in a dirty hand. "How could he do it? Now he will be among the Damned!"

Blanco had been down to the wet shelves —it was where he'd butchered the kid, and he knew how to get there safely. But nothing could be found—only leisurely waves swooping in at him, and sometimes barely wetting the tousled mats of stone where it was said that *los antiguos* had landed in their boats, and sometimes washing sturdily across with strength and depth enough to lift a body and roll it away.

Blanco said to his mother, "It must have been air that he wanted."

The wailing woman repeated, "Air?"

"Yes, yes! He had that fever, and felt so weak, and could not breathe or sleep well in our cave. It was not like our stone shed; then we had two windows. He must have needed to breathe, he thought the sea breeze would revive him. But he crept too far, and so—"

María prayed on, wildly, but she changed the note of her prayers. Soon Blanco observed that she was praying—not for one who willfully and wickedly destroyed himself, contrary to all law of the Church—but for a sad, sick person who had gone crawling as one might go for a stroll, to seek the strong good air.

A body was discovered later that week, farther down the coast near the village of Creta. But it was so damaged by waves and rocks that little could be told except that it was a man.

BLANCO stole, in successive order and mainly from the parked automobiles of rich tourists, a flashlight, a camera, an automatic pistol, another camera, a pair of binoculars.

At first he did not know exactly what to do with these things. He kept them hidden in a cleft high up in the dry cave among fire-blackened walls where his mother could never climb but where he climbed easily.

He had heard bits of gossip about thieves and their ways, at the village, and artfully he tried to lead older boys' conversation toward that subject whenever he went back to watch the boats come in.

Sometimes there was work to be done, and he would be paid in skates too torn to be sold at the market, or perhaps in very small sardines. He had a basket, limp and sodden but still strong enough to carry a load in it, and he would fetch the fish home to María, along with such potato parings and cabbage leaves as he had salvaged behind hotels.

One hot day, when he thought he knew enough about the ways of thieves, he begged for money outside a Megalite café until he had enough for bus fare to Málaga. There was an angry gypsy woman there by the café also, and she cursed at Blanco and tried to drive him away. The *turistas* laughed and thought they were seeing a family fight among gypsies.

So, when he had his fare intact, he caught the afternoon bus in to Málaga. The city was a vast huddle of wonders which petrified Blanco with its noise and immensity. He was frightened to death by streetcars, and nearly run over a time or two. Finally, walking until his bare feet seemed worn through at the bottoms, he found a smelly street called the Calle del Araña Rojo. He walked along this street, carrying the stolen flashlight openly in his hand—playing with it, turning it on and off, casting the light into dim doorways.

A thin young man sitting on a barrel in front of a wineshop: a man with a close-clipped mustache and a soiled pink necktie.

"*Chiquito*, where did you get the flash-light?"

"A man gave it to me."

"Is that the truth? Probably you stole it."

"No, no, I did not steal it. He was a rich tourist; probably he is a North American."

"Where do you live? Where did he give it to you?"

"In Megalite."

"Ah. Let me see the flashlight."

Blanco allowed the young man to finger the handsome silvery thing, but he kept his left hand closed around a rock in his pocket, in case the man should try to run away with the flashlight. Blanco could throw rocks with fantastic accuracy.

"Perhaps you might wish to sell this light?"

"Perhaps."

48

"It could be that I might give you ten pesetas for it."

"That is not sufficient. A small Spanish flashlight has a value of fifty pesetas. And this is an American torch, very large."

"That is true. But I do not wish to keep it. I would buy it from you only to sell it again. I would need to make a profit."

The boy and the young man haggled earnestly. A policeman came by; they left off haggling, Blanco hid the flashlight in his shirt; after the policeman had turned the corner they continued their discussion.

Blanco told the young man—who said merely, "Call me Pepe"—he told him that if he were treated fairly, and not paid in counterfeit money, it might be that he would have other gifts to dispose of . . . gifts from wealthy tourists. He said that the *norteamericanos* were especially benevolent to him.

Finally he gave up the torch for a grand thirty-two pesetas, and took the evening bus back to Megalite. He stopped at the pharmacy and said his mother desired some good medicine which might relieve the pains in her chest. The druggist sold him a bottle of syrupy stuff for fourteen pesetas, sixty céntimos, and Blanco told his mother that a kind lady at one of the luxurious El Remo cottages had given him the medicine when informed that his mother was unwell. Actually the medicine did seem to help María; she had less pain, she felt stronger than before. Sometimes she seemed even a bit tipsy.

All the other "gifts" went piece by piece to Pepe in the Street of the Red Spider; and María marveled at the good fare which Blanco brought home, and at the steady flow of syrupy medicine. Each day she prayed willingly for the generous French and Americans and British who gave pesetas so liberally to her poor son.

Nevertheless the generous French and British and Americans had been outraged sufficiently to appeal both to hotel authorities and to the *Guardia Civil*. Most autos were kept locked, now; an old man patrolled two adjacent parking areas at night; the Guards checked on those cars which were left unlocked in the streets of Megalite, and warned the owners. Furthermore, by midsummer a good share of the foreigners were gone, replaced mainly by Spaniards who drove down from Madrid and Sevilla for seashore vacations. Seldom did these wise people leave such tempting objects in their *coches*.

At fourteen-sixty per bottle the medicine was still a luxury, and María seemed to empty a bottle more rapidly than before. Even though the automatic pistol brought the enormous sum of two hundred pesetas (and a threat from the ugly Pepe that he would arrange to have Blanco turned over to the police unless he agreed to accept two hundred, and not whine for more) the previously stolen goods could not keep the family forever. By July all the pesetas were gone; and the Sanz family had no garden, no fruit to sell, *nada*.

For most of two days and two nights Blanco prowled behind hedges and walls, seeking fiercely for an unguarded, unlocked car. He did find several which it was safe to approach, but in all of them there was nothing to be had except a basket containing children's beach toys. These he took, basket and all, and disposed of them to the man who conducted the local bicycle repair shop and who had several children. Blanco said that he had found the basket abandoned on the beach, and the man generously gave him five pesetas.

After the boy had spent this money for *garbanzos*, potatoes, and a fresh bone and a few spoonfuls of rancid olive oil, he returned to freebooting as soon as his mother had made a stew. Piteously she asked him to seek out the lovely lady at El Remo once more—the lady who gave away big bottles of medicine.

Luck appeared to have come again. Parked in a side lane near the grand Hotel Castillo del Oro was a gleaming red automobile—a convertible, no less. The top was down, no one sat in the car. Blanco went away, only to return ten minutes later, slithering among fig trees across the lane. Midnight, not a soul in sight, and now the last lights in the hotel dining room were turned off.

Without a sound the boy edged barefoot

through the gloom and peered into the back seat. There was a crumpled blanket—covering, apparently, some luggage. No, no—bags he could not steal; he'd realized long ago that he would be seen carrying them. But something which might fit inside his scrawny shirt . . . he opened the glove compartment, and suddenly his breath was taken from him, a trap had closed around his neck. He felt himself lifted and shaken in an agonizing storm. Moaning and mourning, he found himself looking into the dark face of a Civil Guard.

The Guard had hidden himself beneath that blanket in the rear. Now his companion approached jauntily from the hotel parking lot, a fat but handsome figure, remote lights gleaming on his polished hat, on the rifle behind his shoulder.

54

"So you have caught him, Olmedo. Good work!"

Olmedo chuckled. "The credit should really go to you. It was your idea, even if you are too fat to hide beneath the blanket."

"Let's have a look at him!"

Lights blazed in Blanco's face . . . he closed his eyes, there was nothing else to do. The men laughed again.

"Sound the horn of the *coche*, Juan. Then Señor Rata will know that we are finished with it, and he can put it safely away before something is in truth stolen. . . . Or is it that you are the only bandit in this village, *niño?* Are you the one who stole the toys today? Speak up, now, and speak the truth, and avoid a terrible beating! Did you steal those toys in the basket from the car of the Marqués Darrax?"

"*Sí, señor.*"

"And the *pistola* from the car of Señor Whitcomb? That was in March—"

"*Sí, señor,*" he said with tears.

"And the flashlight from the car of Señor Bird? And the camera from the car of Major Maule, the Englishman?"

Blanco admitted to every crime with which he was charged—he even admitted, dazzled and humbled and stricken, to several thefts along adjacent highways which he had never in fact committed.

The Civil Guards lugged him to the long ugly building with its sentries and its flaring red-and-yellow *Todo por Patria* above the door, and after an account of his confessions had been written down he was given bread and wine. Also a cigarette. It was strange but he had never smoked a cigarette before. The *Guardia Civil* laughed heartily when he coughed. His father had never smoked, and Blanco preferred to beg for pesetas or food rather than cigarettes, and he traded off any cigarettes which came his way.

None would be coming his way, not any longer.

(There was hue and cry in Málaga the next morning when officers went hastening to lay their hands on Pepe in the Calle del Araña Rojo. Then the tumult died down and the *policía* were sheepish when they discovered that they already had Pepe in jail, charged with rape.)

María Sanz fainted, after a Guard stalked up the path to the cave and gave her the unfortunate news. The Guard brought her back to consciousness, and made a gypsy take her by *burrito* cart down to her one-time friends in the fishing village. Blanco did not see her again.

He was sentenced to a long term in the nearby reformatory, and the Guards escorted him there. They were greeted by Brother Marco, a great brown-clad bull of a man with a polished pate and a beard the color of blackberries.

He twisted Blanco's ear between his mighty finger and thumb, and made a vulgar sound of disgust.

"First," he bellowed, "you shall have a bath!"

THERE had never been much opportunity for Blanco to play ball before, but now he played *pelota* or *fútbol* nearly every day. Foremost in the riot, capering like a draped ox gone mad, Brother Marco roared over the dry dusty barrens which did duty as a playground. He kept the skirts of his sweat-stained cassock hitched up over the rim of a wide leather belt; he played now upon one team, now upon the other; the slighter figures of inmates strung out like scattered chickens behind him.

Brother Marco's legs were hairy as a goat's and surely, it seemed, as thick as the neck of any goat. He soared with grace: out of the swarm he would lift like a boulder propelled in a blast, and the dirty bare foot and ankle became an instrument of delicacy, kissing the ball with a gentle flash. High and far the ball would go in its sweeping round flight, and Brother Marco would yield up a howl of exultation before his weight struck back against the earth.

The Reverend Father had nominal charge of this reformatory, but he was aged and his thin hands trembled constantly, and he spoke with an uncertain quacking. The other friars worked hard, but when did Brother Marco sleep? It seemed that he never slept.

He was here, there, poking his blunt nose into hot kitchen kettles, bewailing the fact that all the onions were gone . . . Brother Marco loved onions and thought they were good for the boys. But—five pesetas per day, per boy—

He was in the smithy, he was in the long room where they made sandals. He stood with hands on his hips, glowering over the bent scholars who worked in fear or doggedness to correct their illiteracy. (Blanco could read simple printing; José had taught him, with many a thwack and with his rare pained laughter; so Blanco was better off than some.)

Up and down the stairways, through hollow halls plunged Brother Marco. The one worn-out power saw in the manual-training shop spun unevenly on its shaft; this was a

job for him. And when El Pecas nearly sev-
ered his little finger on that same saw, that
was a job for Brother Marco as well.

Did the roof leak above the chapel, did
a driving March storm wrench loose the tiles,
and let rain flow in and loosen plaster above
the shrines? What a sad sight, next morning!
Our Lady was soaked and leaning, and Saint
Francis himself tilted grimly among fallen
candlesticks. But Brother Marco was not
downhearted in the least; and when sullen
voices were raised, questioning why Our Lady
should have permitted this disaster, the big
friar greeted such blasphemy with slaps and
hoarse admonishment.

Anyone could see, he declared: it was a
sign that Our Lady might be wondering
about the sincerity of devotion offered to
Her and to the Saint. Here indeed was a

challenge, a vigorous opportunity for people to prove their reverence and their love.

He led the little band who bore the images to a temporary sacristy. He was up on the roof, fitting new tiles; he was in the chapel, building a mold and shaping plaster, and ordering how the fresh whitewash should be mixed. With half a dozen selected favorites, he polished the few pathetic liturgical adornments until late at night. . . .

Blanco was entranced, Blanco loved Brother Marco, as surely did many another boy. It is unlikely that he would ever have fled the reformatory, no matter how much he longed to be a rich smuggler, had it not been for that big black strap.

It was the friar's own waist-belt (worn calmly in the flaunting of tradition which called for a cord to bind his habit) and it was wide and long and limber and heavy. One blow for a trivial offense, three blows for a deliberate misdemeanor: the breaking of a well-advertised rule. And—oh, *Dios!*— five and six merciless smashes of that fearful weapon against raw and burning flesh: that was for repeated offenses of the same nature. In the case of bigger boys nearly grown to manhood, the floggings could be much more severe. The *pop* of cruel blows, the snarling shrieks punctuating between: these echoed at times along the corridor outside that awful locked door . . . smaller boys like Blanco would go cowering about their business, resolved never to court the strap.

. . . But figs appeared so rich and tempting, swelling among wide leaves in their pear-shaped prettiness. Not often did fresh fruit come to those tables; fruit was too valuable, it could be sold in the market, could

64

be sold for export. Grapes—yes, in season:
sometimes they were donated in response to
prayers.

Brother Marco had laid down the law,
just as he proclaimed it every season. "We
all know," he boomed to a polite audience,
"that there are four fig trees opposite the
playground, close to the schoolroom windows."

The muffled, wordless mumble of assent.

"If one by one we nibble the figs, soon
none will be left, and they will have been
eaten before they became ripe. If there have
to be bellyaches—" he beamed at the vul-
garity— "let us have the bellyaches fairly
distributed! So, no one shall eat a fig until
I examine the trees and announce that the
fruit is ready to eat. Then we will pick the
figs. Then we will divide them fairly. Surely
there will be enough for two or three figs

apiece—possibly even more. Let no boy say that he forgot, or it shall go hard with him."

. . . But the figs hung beckoning in their very fat immobility, they were streaked with violet and darker patches. You looked at the swollen little plummets and you thought of biting through and through, sending your tongue on ahead into the juicy pulp with its tiny jeweled seeds. . . .

Blanco had missed the beach that day. Brother Vicente escorted the younger boys, but Blanco had talked to El Pecas during a period of silence and so was ordered to remain behind and to clean loose stones off the playground, and to be sure that he had collected them all before the beach party returned.

Older youths were in the carpentry shop, working at rush speed to finish a walnut bedroom suite which was on order and behind schedule. Some rich man in Málaga would pay the dizzy total of nine thousand pesetas for that furniture. And the reform school needed new plumbing, the school needed many things.

Brother Marco himself was safely distant in the infirmary, attending a boy who had burnt himself painfully in the foundry: Blanco had seen him striding, armed with bandages and salves.

So who could ever observe Blanco, perched deftly amid branches, seeking out the dainty dark morsels? Fig leaves themselves were more than a traditional concealment—they were a real cloak. Blanco gobbled the first fig—why, it was ripe, or nearly so—and bit into the second.

"For you, Blanco, tomorrow—" That was Brother Marco's voice. The boy nearly fell backward out of the tree.

The friar stood inside the schoolroom window ten feet away. His fierce eyes seemed burning through patterned foliage. "Three blows of the strap! I have no time for you today; I am very busy, with much work to do; but tomorrow— Oh, drop slowly, slowly out of the tree. Do not break your legs. It will do you no good to run, now. Tomorrow, remember: three blows of the strap. Yes, perhaps even four! You have been naughty of late."

. . . So he'd practiced craftily, he'd planned his escape, he'd dreamed of the wealth he would win as a smuggler of cigarettes and soap. Why wait longer, and suffer the strap? No. He'd go this night.

He might even ply back and forth between Africa and Algeciras in a little boat of his own. . . . And a blue motorcycle, or at least a new red scooter, and folds of

money in his pockets. . . . Not only figs
would he buy. He would walk into any
confectionery shop which took his fancy and
buy—not one, not a dozen—but whole trays
of tiny cream puffs, and each with a candied
cherry atop. And the long puffs he had seen
in windows: they were coated with shiny
chocolate, but white cream oozed from their
soft cracks. . . .

So he could leap and he could climb and
he could crawl and he could descend, he
could rush through the night.

He walked the coastal highway, walking
like a country boy going home in lateness,
moving with bounding pulse, and guilt spread
upon his face.

Up loomed the armed might of two Civil
Guards. They were there so suddenly, they
took horrid form in the gloom. Quickly and
arrogantly they must be able to read his

thoughts, to know that he was a runaway, and bound to be a *contrabandista!*

Inmates of the reformatory wore no uniforms. Only shabby ordinary shirts and shorts or pantaloons, and sandals. Blue rags, gray rags, black . . . they wore the garb of poor boys of town or country.

"*Buena' noch'.*" Blanco's feeble lips shook out the words in clipped Malagueñan dialect.

"*Buena',*" said a Guard curtly.

That flashlight upon him once more! It reminded . . . that night in the car, the night he was captured . . . and always he'd feared the *Guardia Civil.* It was their hats, their hats. Shiny, polished wings and membranes rigid and stark: something batlike about them. When he was tiny, a bat had flown in through a window and terrified Blanco on his pallet; it had squeaked as it swept round him. These

70

giant Guards, with their bat-hats and belts and buckles, and one had a submachine gun on its sling. Oh. Bats—

"Boy, where are you going?"

"To find my father."

"Where?"

"He works at the big hotel. Near Creta."

"Ah yes. The Giralda?"

"*Sí, señor.*"

"Where have you been? What have you got here—a towel?" The Guard shook it out, and found nothing in it, and gave it back to Blanco while the boy chattered about his mother; she worked and they lived at the big white *finca* on the Churriana road, and he had gone swimming below the cliffs, and might swim tomorrow at Creta. His mother became sick that evening and sent him—

"Go along, we're not interested in your whole family history. Don't get run over. This highway is dangerous."

So it proved to be. Blanco had traveled less than a kilometer farther when he met up with the French car.

GLARING purplish lights quivered ahead, and Blanco stared in amazement as he walked warily. Before being sentenced, he had moved often on this stretch of road. Then it had been dedicated to silence and rocks—a ragged square of tumbled stone which marked the ruins of a shepherd's hut, a higher sagging column where once the Arab sentinels had strained their eyes seaward. He did not realize the busy expansion in which the Megalite-Creta region now dwelt, with opulent tourists appearing in ever larger invasions.

This new restaurant had been built beside a cliff where the birds used to wheel without disturbance. Its front was adorned with winking shreds. *Vinos, Licores, Bocadillos* read the blotted legend—newly installed but already half defaced. Several cars were parked in a flat area before the wide door; from within the café rang a continuous spasm of guitar music. People were clapping *flamenco* accompaniment as a woman sang loud and shrill.

The French automobile came whining from behind him, boring at high speed toward the west. Blanco turned; he knew at a glance that this was a French car which threatened to run him down. The headlights of American and British and most Spanish

cars were pale, but French cars carried great
frightening torches of purest yellow. He
scooted off the pavement to thorny refuge
among century plants; he had his arm
scratched. But already the advancing car
slowed its speed.

Brakes mourned, tires rubbed pavement,
the car rocked off to the left. Dust whirled
high as it slid to a halt in gravel before the
lurid café. In the silence following its scraping, Blanco heard the laughter of a man and
a woman. They were in the front seat of
this low chariot; the back seat was piled high
with luggage. The car shone lean and gleaming and narrow, built close to the ground
as a turtle.

Blanco was hungry, he would be hungrier
before dawn, and he had not one céntimo,
not one scrap of food in his pockets. The
French never gave as readily as the British,

the British were poorer than the Americans
and could not be so freehanded . . . there
was always a chance.

He trotted rapidly across the road, crunched
his way through gravel, and beside the splen-
did car he made a sound and held out his
grubby hand.

The man wore a blue beret and spectacles,
and had a hard round face. He scarcely
glanced at Blanco. He said with nasal accent,
"Go away, bad little gypsy!"

"Oh, Pierre, *non!*" and past him the woman
beckoned to Blanco, who scurried promptly
around the car to her side. He thought that
she was near to divinity—her pale hair had
blown loose in pure-spun strands from the
scarf which bound it, she wore a fur coat
pulled around her shoulders, Blanco could
smell her perfume in a sugary cloud.

Her lace-gloved fingers lifted a rigid hand-

76

bag—a beautiful thing, that bag, as well as its red-lipped owner—it was made of shiny plastic, filigreed with designs of silver. She snapped open the lid, and drew forth the wealth of nations.

Thousand-peseta notes, folded thick as a tile. The wavering purple glare showed Blanco the engraved figures. Not many thousand-peseta notes had passed before his gaze.

(In the *farmacia*, long before, he was waiting shyly in his rags to buy medicine for his mother. A tan-faced American offered a thousand-peseta note in payment for some trivial purchase, and the wife of the pharmacist rolled up her eyes and gestured helplessly. She sent her daughter flying to the hotel, for change. "But what's so queer about a thousand pesetas?" asked the American good-naturedly. "After all, that's only about twenty-five dollars. In Havana, where I live, that isn't so much." The pharmacist's wife told him, "But in Spain, *señor*, it is a fortune. It is more than many people earn in two or three months.")

He might not tear his eyes from the distraction. He stood in a dream . . . when he became a smuggler, he would have . . .

"I'm sorry." The woman smiled with her narrow, tinted eyes. She spoke in smooth and excellent Spanish. "I thought that I had a peseta for you. But I have no change. Some other time, little boy," and the black lace fingers stuffed back the money and the gleaming gold and silver treasures—wonderful boxes and tubes this lady owned. The plastic handbag snapped shut with a click of finality.

Blanco stood beyond the smear of colored light, watching the man and the woman enter the café. The man leaned heavily against his companion, he put his arm protectingly around her, but was weaving in his pace. A very rich Frenchman, richer than most, and drinking down his gay holiday along with wife or mistress.

At an outside table near the restaurant door, two men now arose, lighted their cigarettes, and disappeared amid the *flamenco* din inside. Instantly Blanco was at their deserted table. They had abandoned half a sandwich and a few almonds and olives. He gathered up this loot and raced off into darkness.

He munched with new contentment and less fear as he strode westward. The olives were stuffed with anchovies, and he savored every joy of delightful pulp before swallowing. The bread made a strength in his stomach the moment it reached it: that strength went on and out, filling his limbs, building eager energy into his thin pace.

How far was Algeciras? A hundred kilometers? Two hundred? It was said to be the gateway to Africa, and from Tangier came all those delights in which the *contrabandistas* dealt.

He might steal a ride on some slow truck as it growled up a grade— For grades curled ahead, hairpins taut among the seaside hills. Mountains were an hour's walk back from the shore at this point, but isolated hills buckled up in blackness from ravines where the slam of surf was very close . . . it was on these salt-stung eminences that *los antiguos* had tussled with their spears and battle clubs: elderly bricks and potsherds were there to prove it.

Few farmhouses had been re-established amid ruins left by the strife of 1936. Kilometer after kilometer the highway ground its curves amid silent shadows where workmen had blasted a floor. The small metal signs of warning were few; when a careless truck driver knocked one down it was seldom replaced. Any idiot should know that danger lurked on each blind turn.

The stiff blank highway flung itself over a ridge, the first twist ending flatly against a wall of shelving clay. It was true that the warning *Peligro* was graven weakly on a lopsided post, but sun and rain and rust had marred the word nearly into vanishment. Truck drivers knew the miseries of these gullies, so did the haughty *cocheros* who piloted blue or scarlet buses. If foreign fools chose to spill themselves amid the shale, why—

Now appeared the French car, identified by twin wands of amber poking out from the vague haze of colored light so far behind. The wands became glass eyes; they stared hard at Blanco, warming the faint mist of salt spray blown around him. Once more he stepped aside to hug the tumbled crannies. The *coche* was humming with increasing speed, it was a gaunt and shiny bullet, it could fling him over the hilltop if it hit his frailness.

His eye caught one snap of a silk scarf, one hasty blotch of man and woman and keen metal as the beast sprang past. Colored headlights hit the claybank, the trap of the descending turn was revealed, brakes began to squawl. The rear end swerved, and a hooting noise leaped dreadfully above a grind of steel and rubber: the soft lady with her perfume and her fur, the lady crying clear.

Rear end dragging the claybank, plowing rubble in a cloud, sparks whorling like flies of fire, the hammer of the car broken with force upon the anvil of a hidden boulder . . . foundry sounds and more sparks. Then the drumming, the bounce and roll far down a declivity that gaped beneath.

Over and over, stiffly turning, the twin wands of yellow light patterned on a farther hill. One went out, there was only one headlight wheeling, slower and slower. Then it snapped off as well; and all the noise and echoes rushed far to right and left, explored among valleys and mountains and ocean clefts, and came again, and in the end receded stubbornly, and died.

. . . Moon rode blandly over recurrent waves; it dressed the raw edges of the cliffs with prettiness. The valley ahead was empty of drumming, devoid of any color save the faintest shred of sudden orange. The sea made sounds, but there was no further sound upon the land save for the *pad, pad, pad, pad* of Blanco's sandals. The boy ran down the curve to where dust still drifted in the half-light.

EXCEPT for a gash in the claybank, there was no visible evidence at the roadside that an accident had occurred. The curves were unfenced, inadequately guarded at intervals by abutments of concrete and half-buried slabs of raw stone. Between two of these the auto had hurtled broadside past a short steep drop, it had rolled into secrecy. Any future headlights boring around those upper turns could not reveal it.

Blanco dropped his legs over the edge and slid through shale until he halted on a more gradual slope.

Directly ahead, in the margin of moonlight but soon to be covered in dense shadows, lay the woman. She had been thrown clear by the initial impact. She was curled amid the flakes of old dynamite blasts . . . moon caught spangles from the rock chips where she was bedded. Her skirts were around her thighs, her scarf was gone, her straw hair spread and waved in the ocean wind. Wetness widened increasingly out from her open jaws.

The boy left her lying there (she cooed like a dove) and he scrambled down the slope to where the hulking car was at rest. He tripped over mutilated bags and strands of clothing as he went; but growing glimmers of orange light were flagging him on.

A fire . . . gasoline . . . once the antiquated auxiliary engine of Pedro Regidor's fishing boat caught fire while men were working on it. Blanco and his father José, with others, doused the fire by hurling handfuls of sand. *Gasolina*, men had cried. . . . Water will do no good! Sand! Sand! . . .

Here was no true sand, but Blanco clawed his fingers into the soil. Arid earth yielded its assistance: shale, pebbles, dirt, dirt, dirt. . . . Sometimes through his frantic scrapings and throwings, Blanco would include bits of dry weed, scraps of leaves. Then the flames widened instantly, hissing and singing until the next volleys of debris battered them out.

It could not have taken two minutes, it seemed that it took two hours. The boy stood gasping, blinking tears from his eyes. No

more licking films of fire, not even any
sparks. Tiny stones kept falling off pipes, off
other portions of smashed mechanism, and
tinkling down through the butchered engine.
There was a steady hiss, the talkative dripping of water and more dangerous fluids,
but only palest plumes of smoke. He had
beaten the blaze.

Words came from beneath the car. But
the talk was in French—words he could not
understand. Blanco crept over boulders between which the wreck was jammed, and
kicked unwittingly against the victim's wide-
flung leg. One flannel leg, gray in the gloom;
one arm, pale hand writhing . . . here was
the head, bald and bloody, and mouthing out
absurd syllables in a continued gasp. The rest
of the man's body was squeezed solid by
the weight of the car.

"*Señor*," the boy whined, "you are not dead?" And yet that was obvious: the man was alive, perhaps he would soon die, perhaps he was dreaming, perhaps he was gone out of his mind with the *coche* pressing him down . . . *ma pauvre Suzy* . . . *ma pauvre* . . . the Frenchman nosed words in a repeated litany.

Blanco was not strong enough to lift so much as an edge of that unwieldy bulk, though he tried. He tugged at the man's arm and leg . . . the man wailed. Blanco shouted a time or two, turning his frightened face up at the empty road; but no traffic passed, and only ghosts of the Ancients could hear him, and fling his plea amid the cliffs in yapping chorus.

Up the slope again, scraping, pawing. Still the woman uttered pigeon noises—but fainter and more tenderly, as if she wished to sleep instead—and he smelled her perfume as he crawled past and bent his fearful glance away from her near-nakedness.

The moon's beams hit at a new angle. They descried for Blanco a small garden of sheerest silver. It was the plastic handbag, splintered among rocks.

Little gauds, metallic squares and tubes, tissues—they were tumbled over a square meter. But under the boy's narrow sole a substance slid as he walked on it, and he looked down. The chunk of bank notes, folded simply, intact.

Insanely he snatched the wad. He fell over a flat boulder, the sleek material clutched in his hand. A fortune . . . pharmacist's wife . . . *one thousand pesetas? It is more than many people earn in two or three months*

. . . he, Blanco, had in his possession a year's salary for a strong and willing man—probably several years' salary.

The bedroom suite at the reformatory's manual-training shop, toiled with and planed and mortised and gilded, month after month: nine thousand pesetas it would fetch in Málaga. Blanco held more than that.

Now stretched the giddy avenue . . . desperate speed, far down the wicked highway to the west, past Fuengirola and Marbella and villages beyond—towns he had scarcely heard of, *pueblos* he had barely guessed at.

He owned enormous wealth, he owned the canny skills which are whetted only by life and death, food-and-starvation necessity. . . . Dispose of these huge bills, one at a time? It would be simple, it would be as the pebble-play of children. Not without absorbing a

thousand crafts and sneaking devices had he
dwelt in the reformatory.

A clean shirt stolen from some family's
spread-out-to-dry laundry, a scrubbed face,
scrubbed hands. The shy, serious trotting into
the big hotel, or even the bank. *"Por favor,
señor.* This large note: Señor Matos has sent
me for change; yes, the owner of the grocery
store. *Cambio, por favor,* in this envelope . . .
muchas gracias."

The woman had no further use for her
money. Doubtless she would die soon, though
not as quickly as José Sanz had died, not as
speedily as Don Miguel Poveda had died, not
as protractedly as María Sanz had died. (Death
throughout Spain, everywhere. It was in the
breeze and the hot sun and the stalking nights,
in sport and in the Church and in salt waves.
Common death—the poorest, smallest boys

recognized it, they stared and shrugged. There had been death for a very long time, there would be a billion new deaths.)

. . . If she did survive, or if the man survived her, what was a fortune in cash to them? They could get more: they owned that broken car, to demonstrate their capacities. They were foreigners, most foreigners were rich, they held vast estates and *fincas* and airplanes, and cigars that cost a day's labor for each cigar, and armies and castles and moving pictures and candy and railroad trains. They owned all, Blanco owned nothing. Until he held this power of engraved paper braced against his beating chest—

These thoughts threw themselves through the boy's mind in a matter of seconds. It was an hour's consideration, a long year's thieving, minced together and squeezed into the briefest fraction of time, as if a ponderous

vise in the carpentry shop had been screwed
to its tightest.

Now he was shocked to the quick at seeing Brother Marco. The friar stood high on
the roadside grade with arms folded across
his cassock; it appeared that he was watching Blanco intently. Was that Saint Francis
accompanying him? Without doubt; and
Blanco went to his knees, scraping his bare
hide below the too-short shorts, seeming to
scrape to the bone.

He crushed the bank notes between his
hands and prayed wordlessly. Tears stung
him . . . one second he could see fairly the
Brother and the Saint, built of solid brown
rock, and watching. A godless creature might
have said that they were merely misshapen
boulders, posted like dolmens by the road
crews to half protect that hairpin turn. But
to Blanco the tall slabs were animate.

One was constructed of sacred gilt and plaster, nerved by every chant which had ever attended . . . the warm halo of the moon was around his kindly skull, the beasts and morning-glories crowded close to let him love them.

And one was solidly earthy and fleshy, smelling of good male sweat, hard-working, tough or amiable by turns, but with a dedication which came forth in resonance between those spectral ridges.

"You would steal from the dead and dying?"

"No, no, Brother Marco! . . . But they do not need—"

"The money is theirs. The need is theirs. Would you leave them cruelly, suffering as Our Lord when He hung upon the Tree?"

"No, no—"

"You would not run with all speed to that

94

café on the road? You would not summon help? You would not seek the *Guardia Civil?*"

"Those bat-wing hats! They are black bats, and I fear their guns and fists, and whips and beatings; and I have run away to be a smuggler; and if I go to the Civil Guards they will seize me as a runaway and lock me up, and you will be summoned, and I will be beaten with the strap . . . bread and water, and no one speaking to me, and allowed to speak to no one!"

"*Deus qui Ecclesiam tuam beati . . . Francisci*—Did Our Lord fear the scourgings and the nails, the thorns impaling His skin? Here is Saint Francis, the dear heart and soul and breath and life of our Order, standing to observe. Ask the good Saint if he feared labor and suffering. *Tribue nobis ex ejus imitatione*—"

95

Shaking with a dry belching spasm, Blanco wiped his arm across his eyes. He peered again. The friar and the Saint had receded into stony silence, but beyond all doubt they watched from other reaches.

He placed the money carefully where he had picked it up; and in that moment, quite unknown to him, the last light at the new restaurant was turned off and the last guest's car went grinding east toward Megalite and Málaga, with the proprietor and his wife following on their motorcycle, and waiters walking home. Blanco was now quite alone on this Golgotha—alone with his conscience, and with whatever determination his ancestors had awarded him.

Blanco crawled up to the pavement and began to run. He ran until his heart was a wild animal inside his slender ribs, until blood burst from his nostrils and covered his chin and shirt. The two patrolling Guards had long since turned aside to scout along cliffside goat-paths, and to rest and smoke in a deserted fold.

Blanco ran all the way to the barracks at Megalite. It was a long run. Even the stern sentinels were impressed when they heard his gulping cry and came hastening to pick him up from the flagstones where he had fallen.

FOR an hour he lay inert on the iron
cot where they jailed him. He watched his
wet shirt flapping in a doorway when the
breeze came through. He heard the truck,
he heard a motorcycle following; he heard
other cars and other excitements. The am-
bulance summoned from Málaga went crying past, and came rushing back. It halted
for a brief check with the Guards, then departed for Málaga with its cargo.

There was a black-mustached man with chevrons on his uniform sleeve. He smoked cigarette after cigarette as he sat watching Blanco. His face was so dark that he might have been a Moor, but no identity revealed itself in the boy's aching mind. Only when Brother Marco walked heavily in, to stand beside the cot with hairy hands spread upon his hips, did Blanco begin to recognize the truth.

"You thought that you would find him here, Brother Marco?"

The boy turned over and covered his head with his arms.

"I did not know. I came to report a run-away. Brother Andrés checked the cells and discovered that he was gone. So I came—"

The Guard smoked on, his voice seemed far away. The boy's sensitive ears could hear the very grinding of his cigarette stub as he put it out.

"Isn't his name Blanco? You may remember—I was the one who caught him in the car, two years ago."

So this same bat-man had returned to manacle Blanco's life, and some especially severe punishment would follow as a result. Blanco was too tired even to cry, even to make the whimper of a bird or a mouse . . . birds, the animals, brothers of Saint Francis . . . voices clung in the air.

"—Another car, tonight," Olmedo the Guard was saying. "Come into the office, Brother Marco, and let me tell you— Yes, I have been promoted. You see I am in command of our barracks tonight."

After a hundred years they came back for their small prisoner. With steady hands the Capuchino drew him from the cot and helped him on with his damp shirt. He guided Blanco into the office, and the two of them stood like fellow culprits before the desk where the hard-faced Olmedo sat in his fierce dignity, with compact and gold cigarette case and lipstick and wallet and thousand-peseta bank notes spread before him for cataloguing.

Brother Marco said, "No one must know of this."

The officer nodded. He lit a fresh cigarette and narrowed his eyes for a time, studying the boy. Blanco was so depressed that he could not even lower his gaze . . . the stiff green red-tabbed figure shivered as in heat waves.

His flat voice spoke agreement. "Yes, Brother Marco. He was resourceful and bold. If the lives of those French are spared they will have this *chiquito* to thank. . . . He has grown taller since he was committed. At first I did not recognize him."

"Perhaps an unidentified country boy

could have observed the accident and reported it?"

"Quite likely."

Brother Marco's hand dropped on Blanco's shoulder with a thud, and the boy shook.

"Come. Let us go home."

. . . Wearily they moved along the dark highway for a hundred meters, then crossed narrow railroad tracks and turned left on the hill road which gave access to a stonier, higher, poorer part of Megalite. This same road thinned itself eventually into the crooked burro path passing the reformatory.

"How did you escape, Blanco?"

The boy told him in mumbling detail. They passed the last blank-walled houses, and heard dogs growling from deeper shadows, and saw starved cats speeding off in front. Moonlight rode cold along with them, making Blanco a weak vassal, a stumbling little

skeleton or slave . . . making Brother Marco
into a ponderous sure-footed thing of gold
and solid shade.

"The wire screen in the smithy?" Brother
Marco mused aloud. "I shall bend that back,
this very hour. There is nothing else to in-
dicate . . . I shall instruct Brother Andrés
. . . no one will ever know."

Blanco gave a sniveling soft cry. "Will
I not be flogged for this? And bread and
water, and no one allowed to speak—?"

"No, no, my boy." In the wan light before the reformatory gate Brother Marco
stopped dead in his tracks, and stood clutch-
ing his huge rosary and praying steadily for
a minute or two.

"Blanco, we have seen a Holy thing. And
you have been a part of it. This is indeed
the work of Saint Francis. Our Lady be
praised! All my life I have hoped to wit-

ness a miracle, and now I have witnessed one!"

He laughed shortly. "Perhaps some day the news will all come out—after many years, when you are old—and a shrine will be erected on the spot. It was Saint Francis in all certainty!"

"Brother Marco," whispered the boy, "I thought I saw him. I—I thought I saw *you*."

"No, child, not *me*. But you might have seen the Saint. Because who else could have drawn you from your bed and guided you over the wall, and past Regina, and down the highway at that particular time and place? On this night—this night, of all nights? You never fled before; I know you will not flee again. You will stay with us here, and in time perhaps you will seek Church Orders. Or you will be a good soldier, *por Dios y por España!*"

He stood huge and exuberant, pointing his finger wildly upward as if indicating angels trooping in the hollow sky. "It was a lonely spot. No one else heard, no one saw. No one but the runaway *niño*, bound to be a smuggler in Algeciras! Had Saint Francis not guided and impelled you, those unfortunate people would not possibly have been discovered until dawn, and then it would have been too late: they would have bled to death. It is a miracle of the most impressive kind, and I only wish that we might share this Holy tale with all the world, now and forever."

He added with practicality, "But we cannot. For disciplinary reasons. . . . Come, Blanco. Into the chapel, and let us pray for the French couple."

On the way Brother Marco halted at the smithy long enough to straighten the old screen which Blanco had bent. Then, before the flower-laden image of the Saint, they remained on their knees for some time, praying that the French should recover their health fully, and giving repeated thanks to Saint Francis and to Our Lady.

Regina came up as they tiptoed into the faint dawn of the courtyard. She sniffed familiarly at Brother Marco's robes, and gazed accusingly at Blanco because he had no more morsels to offer.

"*Chiquito*," whispered the friar, "there is one matter to be established, before I lock you in your cell. Do you remember the three—perhaps four—blows of the belt I promised you?"

"*Sí*, Brother Marco," Blanco answered tremulously. "I was fleeing from them, also."

"But all the school knows of this punishment to come. What will happen to our

discipline if I fail to flog you? No, it is unthinkable that I should neglect. So everyone
must know that the beating has been given."
His whisper was dramatic. "Saint Francis
himself would approve what I plan to do!
Report at the chamber, immediately after
Mathematics in the morning, before you go
to Carpentry."

At the appointed hour and behind that
grim locked door, Brother Marco struck four
violent blows with his big belt; after each
blow Blanco emitted a shrill scream, as he
had been instructed to do. Boys listening in
the outer corridor turned pale and big-eyed,
and stared with fascination at the solid door.

Within the room Brother Marco quietly
shoved back a bench which he had beaten
and then, shaking with silent laughter, he
embraced Blanco and twisted his ear.

Rain and the Feast of the Stars

the

Reiko

Rain and Feast of the Stars

Stars

Hatsumi

DECORATIONS BY JEANYEE WONG

HOUGHTON MIFFLIN COMPANY BOSTON · 1959

Contents

Rain and the Feast
of the Stars

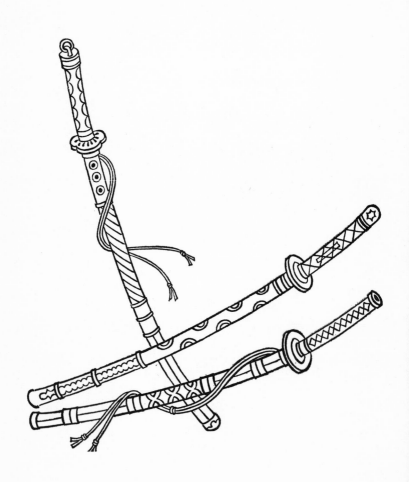

Bahya

"TELL ME a story, Bahya. Tell me the story of Grandmother and the burglar!"

"What, again—Reiko Sama? You have heard it often enough..." said Bahya. But her wrinkled face, across the glowing charcoal fire of the brazier, smiled softly. Sitting there, against the painted sliding doors, she looked like an old statue of Buddha, with her rounded shoulders and tan-colored cheeks, and the light from our paper-framed lantern trembling on her silver-gray hair.

"It doesn't matter, Bahya. Tell it to me again."

"Well then," said Bahya, putting away her needlework, slowly, almost reluctantly, arranging the colorful pieces of cloth one by one into a neat little pile on the matted floor. Around her, around the brown cotton sitting cushion, lay scattered paper dolls, red and black flower cards, and Bahya's old sewing box with its tarnished gilt handle and the lacquered edges peeling. It was quiet in the nursery, except for the crackling charcoal fire, and outside in the dark the sound of frozen rain falling against the shutters, like someone who came to knock, and tiptoed away unheeded.

"When your grandmother came to this house as a young bride," began Bahya, picking up a tangerine and warming it in her hands over the brazier, "I was only sixteen, and very timid. At that time, the government of Shogun Sama had just come to an end, and the world was tumultuous. Bands of burglars went around breaking into wealthy homes, demanding money. They pretended it was for a just cause, which was not true. We all knew it, but what could we do — they were all samurai, skilled in the art of sword handling. After the Restoration many samurai were dismissed from their lords' services, and did not know how to maintain their livelihood except by their swords.

"One day your grandfather went away, and there was no one left in our household but your grandmother and the maids. Here, Reiko Sama —" Bahya offered me a peeled tangerine on a lacquered tray and continued.

"On the fourth day it snowed — it used to snow much more heavily than it does nowadays — and that night burglars came. I was asleep in the antechamber of your grandmother's room. Suddenly I was awakened, and there at my pillow stood two men. Their faces were covered with black masks, and one had a torch in his hand. He pointed a cold, shining sword at my throat and said, 'Don't move, or you will lose your life!' I could hear my teeth chattering. Then one of them said, 'Where is the money? Show us the hiding place!' I didn't know where it was, and fear made me unable to move.

"Just then the paper sliding door opened, and your grandmother stood on the threshold. She was fully dressed, with her hair tied up in a piece of white silk, and holding a halberd in her hand — you know the one that hangs in your father's room. Your grandmother said in a quiet voice, 'What is it that you wish? Please do not frighten our servants, but pray tell me what is your request.' The burglars looked at each other and said, 'We need funds for the Shogun Sama's army. Where is the master of the house?'

"'My lord is away on an errand,' your grandmother replied in a clear voice, 'and there is no one left but myself and my child. If you are not ashamed to fight with a woman, I will accept your challenge in place of my lord.'

"She swung the sword to the level, and came a step forward. Just then the baby began to cry in the next room. One of the burglars turned aside and said in a low voice, 'We do not deal with women or children.' And they left.

"Your grandmother put the sword on the wall, and took the baby in her arms. 'Hush, you are a man. Your father will be ashamed of you.' And she began singing him to sleep. She told me to retire but I couldn't sleep any more that night."

Bahya coughed, and nodded to herself, stretching her trembling fingers over the glowing charcoal fire, her narrow, watery eyes blinking at the days gone by.

"Would they come again, Bahya? Do I have to learn how to handle the sword too?"

"Oh, no, no," said Bahya, stroking my hair. "Those unquiet days are gone. Our Emperor is wise and strong. He will keep the world peaceful for us. Now you will learn only beautiful things. You will learn how to embroider and compose poems, arrange flowers and perform tea ceremony. All those things your grandmother did very well. And you must learn to do them even better."

Bahya thought I looked like Grandmother, my grandmother whom I had never seen. She left this world — oh, so many years ago — and all her belongings were tucked away into a large paulownia chest in the godown. All, except the halberd and the two sets of Sutras that Grandmother hand-copied before she passed away. What was written in those scrolls, bound in faded brocade and lying almost forgotten on my mother's shelf? Bahya said she wasn't sure, because she didn't know how to read. But then Grandmother had once told her that they were about the land she was to go to. A land of crystal flowers and the perpetual spring — a land where five-colored birds sang over the coral pagodas, and each grain of sand was made of sparkling jade...

Some day, said Bahya, some day when I grew up Mother would teach me how to read. Then I could open those scrolls and know more about that blessed land. Some day — but right now I was a little too young.

"Children, children, go and play with the wind," said Mother. "You shouldn't stay inside the house all day, Reiko."

So Bahya and I put on our clogs, and walked out through the wicket side gate to the drowsy back alley, along the sun-speckled mulberry hedge to the open street, the sound of our wooden sandals echoing in the wind.

Hand in hand we went past the lacquer-ware, tea and lantern shops, past the women in cotton kimonos, high chignons and babies tied to their backs, and past the old white dog at the public bathhouse down the block. "Good day," said the carpenter, looking up from his plane stock. "Out to visit the temple again? My, my — may heaven reward such devotion..."

"Not at all," said Bahya. "Heaven should reward you, who work so hard every day."

"Can't be helped," said the carpenter, taking up his tool again. "It's the times, and when you have to feed a family — well, put in a good word for me, Bahya San, when you get to the temple. Maybe I will draw something good at the annual fair."

6. Rain and the Feast of the Stars

Along the Yoko-cho street and over a wooden bridge we went to visit a Buddhist temple every day. Kishi-mojin, dedicated to a demon goddess, was an old temple. Built long before the time when Tokyo was called Yedo, they say, it stood through the changing dynasties and prospered, and when the succeeding regents came hawk hunting with their trains, they used to stop there for a cup of tea. But with the change of time and the gradual decay of Buddhism quietness fell upon the once gaily decked buildings, and the hallowed premises became a children's playground.

Rows of tall oak trees shadowed the winding gravel lane as we walked up toward the main temple gate. At our left stretched a pond where during summer white lotus flowers slept on its still green water. And at our right, underneath the tallest oak tree, stood a small tea house which served roast sparrow and rice wine. Often we stopped in front of the great iron cage in their yard, listening to the chirpings of the soon-to-be-roasted birds. It was a curious contrast, now that I come to think of it — the drunken songs of the young artisans staggering out in their blue liveries, the clamor of the sparrows, and the plaintive chants of Sutras that came floating from the distance...

A little farther along was a shop which sold steamed bean cake and crickets in small bamboo cages. A man with a flowing white beard sat on a stool, his bald head nodding in sleep and quite unconcerned with the hens that hopped around the counter to peck at his merchandise. It was a fascinating shop, with the crickets, and the odd-shaped *ame* candies, and the pink and white cotton cakes encased in glass-topped jars. One day, I couldn't resist the temptation any longer.

"Bahya, couldn't I have one, for once — that cotton cake?"

"Oh, no, heaven forbid," said Bahya. "What would the Mistress say if she heard..."

But the cotton cake looked so soft, and fluffy, with each layer of its silky thread shining in the sun.

"Bahya..."

Bahya stopped, hesitating. She was torn between two loyalties — to my mother, and to me. What would Grandmother have done, in a case such as this? My grandmother who taught her that "No true servant serves two masters, as no virtuous woman takes a second husband..."

"Bahya..."

Slowly her hand went up to her sash, and from the depth of it came out an old hand-woven pouch. Two copper coins fell clinking onto the dusty counter, and the old man, suddenly awakened, bowed several times in hasty gratitude.

"Remember, Reiko Sama, just this once..."

The cotton cake left an airy sweetness in my mouth as we walked up toward the temple gate. Would Mother scold me if she knew? Oh well — the thought was soon forgotten because we could see, beyond the gate, the slanting roofs, red towers, and the Deva gods looming on both sides of the entrance. They were awful figures, those Deva gods — with a sword in one hand, a halberd in another, and an expression of frozen fury on their aged faces.

At the left side of the temple stairs stood a stone wash-basin, old and weather-beaten, with a dozen or so of slender wooden dippers hanging over it, and there Bahya began her ritual. She would cleanse her hands with the somewhat cloudy water, throw a penny into the huge offertory box, murmur some prayers for my health and well-being, then join the circle of nurses from the neighborhood.

Around the empty stone well the old women gathered and gossiped, their low murmuring voices melting into the green shadows of the trees.

"The daughter of the paperhanger, they say, is very ill — I saw a crow fluttering on their roof this morning."

"Then she won't live very long — we'll see the demon fire soon again."

A general shiver and silence — only the soft cooing of the doves flying around the tower. Children played hop-scotch and catchers around the hollow-eyed stone lions, shouting and laughing, their red and blue sashes swinging in the sun.

I wonder how old I was when our trips to the temple came to an end. I was getting tired of the place — of the mournful chants of the beggars who sat around the wooden pillars, of the old bonzes and the young bonzes with their black robes and shaved scalps, and of the never-ending gossip of the trooping nurses around the mossy stone well.

9. Bahya

"I am not going," I said one morning when we were ready to leave for the temple.

Bahya turned around with a black crepe amulet bag in her hand, a puzzled look in her sunken eyes.

"Why — are you feeling unwell?"

"No."

"Don't you want to go and scatter the red beans for the doves?"

"No."

"If Reiko Sama is out of humor today — well, shall we go tomorrow?"

"No."

"Then Reiko Sama would not mind if Bahya went away and left her alone to play all by herself?"

"No."

"It can't be helped, can it?" said Bahya, and stared down at the seam of her worn cotton kimono. "It can't be helped."

From that day on, we stayed at home, spending most of our time in the garden.

Among the high stone walls that surrounded our home we made camellia leis and played housekeeping, or sat beside the pond and watched the golden carp flash through the deep green water. I remember the scarlet *gumi* berries dropping heavily on the wet black ground, persimmons shining in the sun, the reluctant sweetness of *ichi juku* — the fruit without flowers — and the furtive murmur of the stream over the moss-covered rocks. Sometimes we leaned against the stone railing of the bridge and listened to the sound of a *koto* — thirteen-stringed lyre — come wavering through the warm spring dusk. And under the wisteria arbor Bahya made me miniature gardens with tiny shrines, red round bridges and shining sand streams.

In the southwest corner of our garden stood a warehouse, where we kept old armor, scrolls and lacquered furniture. A big white snake lived behind it, and every fine day I saw him sunning himself on the steps. It was fun, sometimes, to throw pebbles at him to see the flicker of light in his tiny red eyes. But Bahya revered him very much.

"Don't make him angry," she would say. "He is the guardian deity of this house — he keeps all the evil spirits away."

Being a staunch Buddhist, Bahya believed in reincarnation, and would not kill even an ant. "Be careful, Reiko Sama," she often said. "Who knows, you might be stepping on one of your ancestors." And if I did not behave myself in this world, even I too might be transformed into an animal or an insect in my next life — which was a frightening thought.

"But Bahya is so superstitious," said Mother. "I am afraid the child will grow up with her head full of silly notions."

"Don't worry," said Father, as calm and imperturbable as usual. "She will grow out of it soon enough — the others have. Besides, Bahya has been with us for such a long time."

"I am not saying that she should go," Mother replied

a little irritably. "It's only that I think it's about time we had someone else..."

A backward child, always hiding behind Bahya's sleeves. A child so shy that she can't even greet the guests — that's what Mother said about me, and perhaps she was right, because I could never get used to strangers, and my tears came very easily.

Once a month a tea ceremony was held at our home. Early in the afternoon Bahya would dress me in my best kimono with embroideries of seasonal flowers, comb my straight black hair, and say, "Now, Reiko Sama, I beg you not to wear a long face today. Baroness Tsukugawa and Mrs. Maeda are going to be here, and they will want to see a nice, well-behaved little lady." Then she would take my hand and lead me through the long dark corridor to our tea room. I remember standing in front of the gilded sliding doors, tracing with my fingers, feeling reluctant and rebellious. The long silk sleeves felt heavy on my arms, and the tight brocade sash was suffocating. I still recall with panic the rows of smiling faces against the golden screen, hum of polite conversation, the scent of aloe wood, and the bitter fragrance of the thick green tea.

"Greet the guests, Reiko," Mother would say. "Your bow is still too high — she really hasn't learned her manners yet..."

Then: "My, how big you have grown..."

"What a lovely kimono..."

"Such beautiful hair — and so quiet..."

And then, "How old are you?" from Mrs. Maeda, a

stern-faced woman in a dark brown silk kimono. She never seemed to remember how old I was.

"Tell Mrs. Maeda how old you are, Reiko," Mother would say, a little impatiently. "You should answer properly when you are spoken to."

What could I say to those formidable ladies? I feel confused and miserable, and my face grows hotter and hotter. So I keep silence, staring down at my sleeves lying heavily on the matted floor, trying not to cry.

"All right," Mother says, giving up. "You may go, Reiko Chan."

How wonderful it was to be back in the nursery, with my *papier mâché* dogs, twill dibs, woodcut picture books, and Bahya squatting in the sunny corridor, her thin shoulders bent over a new silk kimono for my doll.

So the world I lived in was like the miniature garden Bahya made me. We were the only inhabitants there, with our toys and the flowers and the little round red bridges, and as I grew, it was Bahya's ideas, fears and superstition that shaped and molded my dreams, and became a part of my life — like a lacquered thread in the pattern of brocade.

And I thought it was going to last forever, our little world.

"Mother, where did Bahya go?"

"Ah, Reiko. I didn't know you were there. Bahya went to visit her relatives. Now go and play with Kiyo, and don't make too much noise."

I didn't know Bahya had any relatives, I thought,

slowly walking away from Mother's room, down the corridor in search of Kiyo. Bahya said she had a nephew, but then she went to visit him only once a year. And it was always at the time of *Bon*, the feast for the dead. Or was the nephew dead? Perhaps...

The maids were picking plums in the back yard.

"Reiko Sama is lonesome because Bahya is away," said Kiyo, wiping her purple fingers on her apron and smiling. "If you would be patient for a while, Kiyo will make you a plum pickle stick."

Sitting on a white porcelain stool and sucking at the plums I listened to the maids chattering. Soon they forgot that I was there.

"What I don't understand," said Toki, gathering up the pale green plums in a basket, "is that she is so stubborn about it."

"Did the Mistress say anything to her?" asked Kiyo.

"No, but she must have overheard something. And she thinks she will be out of place when the new one comes."

"What's that got to do with her — that things change from time to time? We all have to go along with the ways of our masters. Besides if she stayed here, our Mistress would even give her a nice funeral — she wouldn't have to worry about a thing."

"What is su-per-stition?" I asked.

"My, my, Reiko Sama is indeed a clever little lady," said Kiku, laughing. "Where did you learn such a long word?"

"Mother."

"Is that so? Well, superstition is believing in what is not true."

"What is not true?"

"Yes, Reiko Sama. Like Bahya when she doesn't eat meat because she thinks heaven will punish her for it."

"Oh..."

The plums tasted sour, and I had to swallow. A little breeze went by, and an orange-colored ladybug crawled across my feet. The clouds were turning red in the western sky, and on the ground the far-reaching shadow of the *basho* tree fell, black and jagged and faintly trembling.

Like Bahya...The plum stick fell softly among the grass as I slipped off the porcelain stool and wandered away. Away from the maids and the back yard.

Slowly, almost imperceptibly, the dusk was gathering on the lawn. At the farther edge of the garden trees stood, the tips of their high branches still shining in the sun, but across the pond, at the foot of the mound, crouched the pines, silent and menacing in the pale evening mist. Everything was still, even the tiny stream underneath the bridge.

Where did the water go? I wondered, staring down at the dry river bed. It all went down to the pond, singing, only yesterday. But now, instead of the water, twisted branches lay scattered among the pebbles, dark brown and lonely looking.

A shadow fell on the stone railing of the bridge, and a familiar voice called me. "Reiko Sama." I turned around, almost jumping.

15. Bahya

"Bahya, Bahya, you came back!"

"Of course I did," said Bahya, faintly smiling, her sunken eyes gleaming like two little pools underneath her brows.

"You won't go away again, will you, Bahya?"

"No, Reiko Sama," said Bahya, quite firmly, then added half to herself, "Not if it is what Buddha wills..."

Shadows deepened around her thin bent shoulders as she turned away, fumbling with her brocade money pouch. "We must go in, Reiko Sama," she murmured. "It's almost suppertime."

"But why, Mother — why is she leaving?"

"Bahya is old, Reiko Chan. And she wants to have some rest now."

"But why — can't she stay here and rest?"

"Bahya is going to live with her nephew, Reiko. It's just like being with her own family, you see."

Her own family — but no, that couldn't be. Bahya belonged to us, wasn't that what Grandmother said? Besides, who was going to take care of my crickets while I was away in summer — and who was going to tell me stories when I went to bed? Bahya said she wouldn't go...

"She might have," said Mother, losing patience. "But she's changed her mind now. She says she wants to go, and there's nothing we can do about it." There was a tone of finality in her voice.

The day when Bahya came to say goodbye I was playing in my mother's room. Hana, one of the upper maids, came to announce her. Then behind the half-opened sliding door I saw Bahya squatting, in her best black silk kimono, both hands on her lap.

"I beg your pardon," she said, and bowed very low, till her little gray chignon brushed the matted floor. "I have come to take my leave," she mumbled. "Thank you so much for the kindness I have received in this household. And please forgive me for all my faults and shortcomings."

"We have asked you not to go," said Mother. "But since you are so intent on leaving us, we cannot force you to stay either. Anyway, you may feel free to come back whenever you wish. And let us know if you ever feel in need of anything."

"Thank you so much," Bahya bowed again.

"Don't go," I said.

Bahya looked up, her eyes blinking under the wrinkled lids.

"But I must go, Reiko Sama," she said quietly. "Before long Bahya will be of little use to you. You must study hard and become accomplished. Please be a gentle, great lady like your grandmother." Bahya sounded proud and strong as she said the last words.

Under the high tiled ridge of our gate I watched Bahya go away. The jujube tree near the hedge smelled bitter and a little musty like Bahya's cough medicine. And next to it *yamabuki* was bursting into tiny yellow buds. Plucking at them one by one I watched her little

17. Bahya

bent figure grow smaller, with a string of black beads in one hand, a bundle in another, walking with small, unhurried steps. The rhythmical *karakoro-karakoro* of her wooden clogs sounded "Can't be helped, can't be helped."

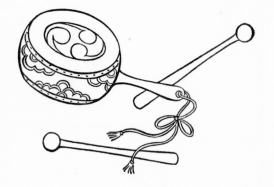

Dolls'
Festival

THE FIRST clear realization of what was to happen came on the day when I went to bed with a cold. My nursemaid was away, and Mother had a guest. I didn't feel well at all, and made things very difficult for poor young Hana. My father heard about it, and ordered me to be brought to his room. "I will watch over her," he said. "It will be better than being alone in the nursery upstairs."

Lying between layers of thick feather quilts I stared up at the high, dark, tessellated ceiling, twisted ebony pillars, gently curving swords on the rack, and the curious, colorful pattern on my silk coverlets. It was late November. Outside, *kogarashi*, the tree-withering blast, howled mournfully. Father sat, silently writing at his red sandalwood desk, his mustached profile dark against the white paper screen.

Mother must have come in while I was asleep, and half awake, I listened to her voice, serious and respectful, addressing Father. "I regret very much that I have to disturb your studies," she was saying. "But this is an important matter which I cannot decide alone."

"Well," said Father.

"After all, Mariko has come of age. And Mr. Kido says the other party is very anxious for the arrangement."

"Well," said Father.

"They say they are not even objecting to her being a Catholic."

"Oh?" he sounded indifferent.

"It's not that we are sending her away against her wish — she knows she will have to go sooner or later."

"Well," said Father.

"I do not particularly want to marry her off so young and let her face the hardships, but in a way it will be easier . . . She will have less difficulty adjusting herself to the new household."

"Well."

"It pains my heart to see her go — such a gentle, obedient child. And I have taken such care all these years to bring her up." Mother sounded very sad. "But the more I feel for her, the more I hope to find a suitable household and settle her future securely before anything happens to either of us."

"Well," said Father, still writing.

"I cannot do anything with you saying 'well,' 'well' all the time." There was a trace of annoyance in Mother's voice. "You can indulge in your studies all day and let the responsibility fall on my shoulders. But please think a little in my place — with a daughter old enough to be married..."

Father laid down his pen and looked at Mother, with a light of amusement in his eyes. "What do you want me to do — we can't very well advertise in the newspapers. Or shall we say, 'A daughter of marriageable age on this part, personal appearance average but guaranteed for quietness'?"

Mother smiled, half resentfully. "That is why I am asking your opinion about this family — I have been for the past hour."

"Oh, I see, you should have told me in the beginning. Women are so roundabout — it takes an hour to unfold anything."

Quietly, Mother placed a photograph and some papers on his desk.

"Let me see — Senior grade of the third rank, First Order of Merit, age fifty-seven...It appears to me he is a little old to be looking for a bride."

"Please — that is his father!"

"Oh, I see. Wait — wait, I know the man. An excellent family — but I hear has something to do with the Manchurian Railway. A pity, such an old family, in trade..."

"We can't be bothered about such things nowadays. How would you consider this match?"

"Well, I should think everything depends on the desires of the party concerned. If Mariko wants to go, let her go. If she doesn't, there is no need for hurry."

"But there *is* need for hurry — otherwise I wouldn't be so concerned. When I think that she is the oldest of our daughters..."

The painted sliding doors opened quietly, and a maid' knelt on the threshold. "Reiko Sama's doctor has arrived," she said with a bow.

Several weeks later, my sister was called to the detached study where Father worked. And that evening when Kiku came up with my supper tray she told me there was going to be an *omedeta* — a joyful event — in my home. "Mariko Sama is going to become a bride," she said, smiling mischievously.

"When?"

"We don't know yet. Reiko Sama must wait until our Mistress mentions it — please don't say I told you."

"I will ask Onesama — honorable older sister — then."

"Sh — don't do such a thing!"

"Why?"

"She will be embarrassed."

I didn't see why one should be embarrassed by such a joyful event, so the next morning after breakfast I wandered down to find my sister. But there was no one in her room. Only a little white rice bird twittered in its cage, hopping from perch to perch in the weak yellow sun. A faint smell of musk clung in the air, and in the shadowy corner a slender clothes rack of rusty vermilion shone dimly. No one seemed to have sat on the damask-satin cushion placed on the matted floor; no one had touched the drooping goat willow on the dais that morning.

Wondering where my sister could be, I knelt down beside her writing desk. Everything was in its place as usual — a shining letterbox inlaid with gold, with crimson tassels of silk, a calligraphy set in varnished brown, a small ivory statue of the Virgin Mary, and a string of crystal beads that belonged to my grandmother.

Beside the bamboo brush stand something square and flat, neatly folded in white paper caught my eye. I took it up, hesitated, then without opening the wrapping placed it on the desk exactly as it lay before I touched it. I knew what it was — a photograph of the bridegroom, my older sister's future husband. Suddenly, I felt as if I were doing something wrong being in her room, alone, while she was away. The quietness of the room, and the little white statue made me feel like a stranger.

Perhaps I shouldn't ask her anything, I thought, slowly climbing the polished wooden stairs to my nursery.

Weeks passed, but there was no change in my sister's demeanor. As usual she played the thirteen-stringed lyre, arranged flowers, embroidered cherry blossoms on a black satin cloth, and read her favorite poems from the classics. Then finally the day of the formal meeting came.

She looked beautiful that morning — in a deep lilac kimono with white peonies blossoming out on the hem, her long, shiny black hair drawn back in a neat little bun, coral brooch on a brocade sash, and a touch of powder on her slight oval face.

"*Itte mairimasu* — I shall go but to return," she said, tipping her head a little to the side, as she always did when speaking to people.

"If you don't like the way he looks, say so frankly," said Father. "No use being bashful about such things."

My sister blushed, and turned away.

That evening Mother looked thoughtful. "It's an important decision, Mariko San," she said. "So think well over it. If you don't want to go, it is not too late to refuse..."

"I — don't know, Mother," my sister replied hesitantly. "I hoped — to stay home a little longer. Perhaps..."

"But remember, Mariko San," interrupted Mother. "A woman has to get married sooner or later, for that is her duty. You might be happy, and then again you might not be. But in life..." Mother stopped, as if searching for words. Then she added, a little sadly, "In life — a woman cannot expect too much happiness. So think it over carefully, Mariko San."

"I would rather leave it to you and Father," my sister answered in a low voice. "I would rather not decide by myself..."

I heard no more about the marriage, while New Year's feast came and went. Pale sasanqua flowers withered and dropped away. Scarlet nandin berries shone in the frost-bitten sunshine, and the green jonquil leaves grew inch by inch on the shadowy dais. Plum blossoms began to spread their fragrance in our corridor, and with the flowering of the peach trees the dolls' festival came.

Early in the morning of March the third, Jiiya, our old manservant, set up the five-storied dais in our back parlor and covered it with a crimson rug. The maids brought different-sized paulownia boxes from the godown, and with Mother's help we took out the little dolls from their yellow silk wrappings and placed them one by one on the steps.

It was a lovely scene, with the Empress in her dress of silver brocade, holding a coral fan in her tiny white hands, and next to her the Emperor on his ivory throne, with an ebony scepter and a crown of gold. Beneath them were the lords and ladies in ceremonial robes, their fans and swords shining in the flickering candle-light — then the warriors in scarlet armor, with bows and arrows on their backs, white horses, lacquered saddles, musicians playing their flutes, lyres and drums, paper-framed lamps and tiny mandarin trees...

Finally a table laden with wine cups and different-colored rice cakes was brought in and placed in front of the dais.

"You had better all go and change," said Mother. "The guests for the luncheon should arrive very soon."

"Just a second," said my sister, striking a match. Then putting the light in two miniature hand lamps, she slid back on the matted floor and gazed at the pageantry.

"It's too early for that," said Mother. "You'll have to wait till the guests are here."

"Yes, Mother," my sister replied obediently. "I just wanted to see how it looked with the lamps on, before people came."

The tiny flames glowed warm and cheerful in their white paper frames. Little musicians with shaved blue scalps played on in silence. And against the gloom of our back parlor the dainty white-faced dolls stared ahead, immobile and unconcerned, glittering in their cloth of gold. Hesitantly, my sister blew off the lights, shielding the lamps with her sleeve. Then without a word she left the room.

With each rain the weather became warmer. The formal exchange of *yuino* — betrothal presents — took place, and Mother was busy preparing the trousseau. Day after day new sets of furniture arrived, and soon our parlor was filled with paulownia wardrobes, lacquered chests and clothes racks, colorful silk quilts, and mosquito nets. Clothes merchants wearing blue cotton aprons, seamstresses with leather thimbles, dyers and embroiderers streamed in and out of our gate, and gradually the wardrobes became filled with layers and layers of kimonos — some with our paulownia crest on, some plain — pink, light blue, deep purple, dyed ones, embroidered ones, hand-painted ones — with gold, silver, lacquered threads of deep red and black — cherry flowers for spring, plum blossoms for winter, iris for early June, goldfish pattern for midsummer, and chrysanthemums for autumn. Yards of brocade were sent from Kyoto, some brilliant, some somber, and finally a set of hair ornaments made of spotless tortoise shell arrived. Clear amber-colored and delicately wrought, it looked like a whole seven-roofed pagoda in elaborate miniature. In the hallway presents from our acquaintances made a small mound, and merchants, shopkeepers, artisans and local firemen came one after another to offer congratulations. But with the approach of the joyful day, my sister grew even more silent.

The evening before the wedding I went into her room, hoping she would play with me for a while before supper. She was sitting alone on the matted floor, staring vacantly at the garden. The soft, golden glow of the clouds reflected on her hair, gently sloping shoulders, and the white hands folded on her lap.

"Onesama," I called hesitantly.

She stirred, and turned around. "Ah, Reiko Chan," she murmured, standing up. "Would you like to come with me for a while?"

"Where?"

"To the garden."

The sky was turning pale blue. The shadow had begun to gather among the tall *mandala* trees, and somewhere far, a temple bell rang the setting sun. We walked across the lawn, through the flowering azaleas, and stopped at the curving bridge over the stream. Through the pine trees the water of the pond gleamed black and bottomless. Only from time to time a large carp jumped, falling with a splash onto the still surface.

"It's too early for *hazumiso,* isn't it?" my sister said. "It's too dark to see anyway." Remembering that every year we used to look for the tiny blue berries hidden deep in the bladelike grass, I asked, "Shall I get some candles and matches from Kiyo?"

"Oh, no." She smiled. "I just wondered, that's all. Besides, I have matches..." I looked back at our house. The lights were on, and shadows of the maids went about busily through the corridor, in and out of the brightly lit dining room.

We walked around the pond and came to a tall stone lantern with a hollow top. "Wait just a minute, Reiko Chan," said my sister, and took out a bunch of papers from her sleeve — letters, scraps of poetry, and a diary. Bending down, she stacked them on the ground and struck a match. A little blue flame went up and cast a trembling light on the smooth white surface of the lantern, turned orange, then died down. Still kneeling, she watched the papers turn to curling black ashes.

"Shall we go?" I asked, getting bored. She stood up, and with one hand straightening the fold of her kimono, took my hand with the other, and slowly started back.

"Onesama," I tugged at her sleeve. "Why did you burn those papers?"

"Because I have to go away tomorrow."

"Will you be able to come back often?"

"No, not very often."

"Do you have to go?"

"Yes, I have to."

"Because Mr. Kido brought the wedding presents?"

My sister smiled again. "Precocious child," she said. "Who told you?"

"Mother."

"I see," she said, and dropped my hand. "I wonder," she added slowly, frowning a little, "if Mother and Father are always right...Even if they weren't, I suppose they can't help it. For it's what they believe the only way..."

I stopped and looked up to her face, not understanding what she was saying to herself. "Onesama," I said. "Why do you look so sad? Do you have a headache?"

"No, I don't have a headache," she said gently. "And it's no use being sad."

"Why?"

"Because there are things everyone else expects you to do, and you can't always say no."

"Why? Why can't you say no?"

"Because even if I could say no, I wouldn't know what to do afterwards...You'll understand when you grow up."

"I don't think I want to grow up, ever," I said, pouting.

"I wish I didn't have to either," my sister said. "Now run along and wash your hands and face. Don't forget to ask Hana to comb your hair too."

There was not a speck of cloud in the warm blue sky the next day. "Very unusual," said Mr. Kido. "Very unusual. In late April we generally have flower-gloom. This is indeed a good omen. Well, well, it's going to be a busy day. Pardon me, everyone, I have to rush..." No doubt it was a busy day for my sister — Mass at the Cathedral in the morning, reception for the guests, official registration in the afternoon, then later the announcement banquet at the Imperial Hotel.

When my other sister, my brothers and I arrived, the banquet hall was more than half filled with guests. Under the crystal chandeliers men in tail coats stood around, glasses in their hands. Elderly ladies in black silk kimonos, young girls in brightly colored robes and brocade sashes nodded and smiled at each other. From time to time waves of discreet laughter went across the heavily scented air. In the soft half-light, waiters in tuxedos tiptoed around, solemnly offering cocktails and imported sherry. At the entrance my sister stood with her husband, dressed in white ceremonial kimono with floating silver pattern of tortoise and crane. She looked pale, and her elaborate hair style with its pins and tassels seemed almost too heavy for her. The tall, thin bridegroom stood erect in his black Western clothes and bowed his head stiffly to the incoming guests.

How many hundreds of people there were I don't remember when we finally sat down at the banquet tables. From my place in the corner I could look down over the sparkling glasses and clusters of carnations to the center where my sister sat, now in a different costume of brightly embroidered silk, her head bent down and scarcely lifting her fork from her plate.

"Why isn't Mariko Onesama eating at all?" I whispered to my brother who sat next to me. "I wonder if her sash is too tight?"

"Silly," said my brother. "Brides aren't supposed to eat — not much anyway. How can she — everyone gaping at her like that."

Course after course followed. Wines were poured.

Glasses were emptied, and filled again. Soon after the desserts were brought in, Admiral Hori, dressed in full uniform, stood up. Table speeches were beginning.

"Ahem," said Mr. Hori. "Unworthy as I am, having been appointed the official go-between..."

Oh dear, I thought. Poor sister — she must be frightfully hungry.

From time to time stray words came into my ears. "The groom has graduated with honors from the Tokyo Imperial University — unmatched talents — highly intelligent — cheerful disposition — skilled in modern sports — a brilliant future in the government. The bride is a graduate of Sacred Heart Normal School — unparalleled in wits and beauty — various accomplishments, of which she excels in the art of poetry — docile, gentle, refined..."

I looked down toward my sister again, and my new brother-in-law, both of them looking down, silent and detached. Somehow, the burning colors of her kimono, shining ornaments, and their white, immovable faces made me think of our last dolls' festival. The only difference was they didn't have to go back to their paulownia boxes and then to the dark godown, there to be forgotten for another year...

Finally all the guests left, with much congratulations, handshakes and bowings. It was close to ten o'clock when my sister came down to the lobby with her coat and shawl, ready to leave. I was getting very sleepy in a soft armchair, forgetting everything that had happened.

"Goodbye, Reiko Chan," said my sister.

"Goodbye — good night," I said, waking up. "When

are you coming home?" But she was walking away toward the entrance, with her husband and his family — followed by mine, which was no longer hers.

A shining black car waited outside. My brother-in-law bowed to my parents and got into the car, while the chauffeur held the door open. My sister turned around to follow him in silence. "Just a minute, Mariko San." Mother stepped forward to adjust my sister's shawl from behind. Mother's hand touched her shoulder. Suddenly, with a small, irritable motion my sister jerked Mother's hand away. "Please don't," she said in a tiny, choking voice, and quickly stepped into the car. My brother-in-law bowed stiffly through the dimly lit windowpane. My sister's face was turned downward, her eyes almost closed. In silence we watched the car glide through the hotel gate, away into the streaming city lights. "Mariko was such a gentle child..." murmured my mother. "Such a gentle child." There were tears in her eyes.

Etsu and the Snow Woman

"This is almost like home," Etsu said. She was knitting a pair of pale blue socks for me. "Only it snows much better there."

"How better, Etsu?" But she was busy counting the stitches. The sky looked pearly gray through the frozen windowpane. Large cotton balls of snow fell into our garden, quietly, incessantly, hiding everything under a thick, white, feathery quilt. Across the lawn the pines and the willows stooped under their silvery load. The ice-covered pond had long since disappeared, and the stone lantern looked taller topped with snow. Little shiny flakes clung to the thin black ropes of my swing, and the round *sharinbai* tree sat like a huge round teacup floating on a soft white sea.

Even inside the house we could see our breath come out in transparent puffs of cloud, and Etsu's hands looked red and cold. But under the cover of a flowered quilt hung over the sunken brazier it was very warm, and the little snow rabbit on the lacquered tray was gradually melting away. From time to time burning charcoal sputtered in the new black ash, and the yellow ginko-fruit peel in the fire smelled oddly sweet and stinging.

"How better, Etsu?" I asked again. Etsu stopped her busy fingers and looked up with a smile on her pale white face.

"It snows much, much more, Reiko Sama. And then, we go to school on skis and sledges."

"And then?"

"Then we have to come home because it gets dark early, and if you stay out too late, the Snow Woman will come to get you."

"What would she do?"

"She will give you her milk, and when you drink, you forget everything—your father, mother, your home, and the Snow Woman will take you far away into the mountains."

"Will she come into our garden too?" I looked out into the garden again, to the gentle slope of the mounds, curling brushes of bear-bamboo near the sedge, squatting snow lantern and the curving stone bridge, all hidden under the thick white snow. "Will she take me away, Etsu?"

"No, Reiko Sama," said Etsu. "Hokkaido is far away ..."

Etsu was my new nursemaid who came after Bahya had gone. I was getting too old for Bahya, but I was too young, Father said, to have a real governess yet. So Etsu was sent for, all the way from Hokkaido, traveling days and nights, on road and sea.

Hokkaido must be a strange land, I thought. It was far away in the cold and dark North, full of big black bears, snowy mountains, and the hairy people called Ainus. And there in one of the snow-covered cities my oldest brother studied about those odd people. Etsu, however, wasn't an Ainu. She was thin, very white, and had a small silvery voice. "She seems like a nice girl," wrote my brother from Sapporo where he attended the university. "And well educated. She will make a good companion for Reiko."

Being well educated, Etsu wasn't superstitious like Bahya. Instead, she often talked about her home. She talked about the new, clean, spacious cities, big plains, the dark, gray, angry northern sea, and the high mountains always covered with snow.

"But it doesn't snow all the time, Reiko Sama," said Etsu, taking up her knitting again. "In May the apple trees begin to blossom, and soon after that, whole fields and valleys will be covered with tiny white bell orchids. And on an early summer morning you can see black shadows of young colts racing through the mist on the green meadows."

36. Rain and the Feast of the Stars

My hands under the silk coverlet, I watched Etsu knitting. Her thin white face bent down, her narrow black eyes intent on her work, she seemed to be thinking about something far away.

"Do you want to go home, Etsu?" I asked, not knowing quite why.

"No, Reiko Sama," answered Etsu, bending down still lower. "Heaven would punish me if I thought of such a thing — being allowed to stay at a household like this..." After a pause, she put away the half-knitted sock and stood up. "I must take the snow rabbit away — it's all melted to water." Taking up the black lacquer tray, she left quietly.

The next morning, sun shone brightly on our all-white garden. It shone on the snow-covered pine trees, it shone in the icicles hanging from our eaves, and it shone on the maids' hairpins as they went about on their high wooden clogs, thrashing snow off heavily laden willows. The sky was blue and cold. A slight wind was rising, and from time to time it blew up a cloud of snow that sparkled like flakes of gold in the bright winter sunshine.

"Rare snowfall," said Jiiya, our old manservant. "I thought I felt the chill much more severely in my bones this winter."

"I don't think it is so cold, Jiiya San," said Etsu, smiling. "But then I am used to the weather in Hokkaido..."

"Speaking of Hokkaido, when is the young master returning from school?" asked Jiiya. "It's about time we saw him again. Have you heard anything from your home, Etsu San? He stops at your father's store at times, doesn't he?"

Etsu said she didn't know, blushing a little.

"Did you bring me back something nice? Did you bring me back a bear cub as you promised?"

Holding me up in the air, my oldest brother laughed. "My, how heavy you've gotten. No, I didn't bring back any Ainu or bear cubs. Only photographs of the mountains I climbed and an onyx brooch for you. Have you been a good child and nice to Etsu? I'll be scolded by her parents if you weren't, you know."

I nodded, still sleepy. I had just gone to sleep when my brother came home, and insisted that I should be awakened and brought to the parlor, for he wanted to show me the pictures he had taken. All my family was gathered around the large brazier, everyone except Father. Maids were serving hot green tea and rice wafers, and Mother buried some chestnuts around the glowing charcoal fire. My brother was snow-burnt almost to black, and his teeth gleamed white when he laughed. There were many pictures scattered on the matted floor — some with my brother in them, some of his friends, and some just the range of high, beautiful mountains. He told us of the wide and lonely plains where there lived only bear and wild fowl, and of the dark and endless forests.

"These mountains look very steep," remarked my mother, taking up one of the photographs. "Isn't it dangerous to climb them?"

"Not if you are careful," said my brother. "Of course

there are always accidents, but that's the chance you have to take."

Mother sighed, putting down the photograph. "Every year you come back with more pictures," she said. "And the mountains in them get higher and steeper. I wonder —" She paused. "Someday, something might happen to you, and then..."

The sliding door opened and Hana placed her hands on the threshold. "The master waits for you," she said with a bow. A cloud crossed my brother's brow. He said resignedly, "I suppose I should go right away — shouldn't I, Mother?"

"Of course, Kazuo San," replied Mother, stirring the chestnuts in the hot cinders with wrought-iron fire tongs. "You should have gone before he asked for you."

"Come, Reiko Chan." My brother put me on his shoulder and marched down the corridor, singing. As we approached Father's study, we could see his shadow on the paper door, absolutely still and a little lonely. My brother put me down and opened the sliding door very gently.

"I am back, Father," he said.

My father turned from his desk. "So I see," he said. "How is school?"

"Fine, Father."

"You have been studying hard, I hope?"

"Well — yes, Father."

"Very well then," Father made a slight move as if to turn away, then changed his mind. "By the way," he added casually, "how about making the round of New

Year calls for me? If you don't mind, I will have the list of names and addresses made out for you."

My brother opened his mouth to say something, hesitated, and said, "Yes, Father."

"Good," said Father. "It's time you learned something about the duties of an eldest son. Good night."

"Good night, Father."

My brother did not sing as we went back to the parlor, hand in hand this time, down the long, cold corridor...

As the year drew to its end, our household grew very busy. Every sliding door was dusted, every mat carefully wiped. Out in the back yard Jiiya, our old manservant, hoisted red and yellow buntings around a large wooden hand mill, and the heavy sound of pounding rice dumplings echoed in the frozen winter sky. In the alcove of our sitting room boxes of presents bound with gold and silver threads were stacked high. Mother was busy addressing hundreds of greeting cards, and Etsu went away from the nursery to help her. In the kitchen maids prepared dishes for the coming New Year festivities, and our dining room table became laden with black lacquer food boxes inlaid in gold.

The Yoko-cho street was crowded with busy shoppers. From the brightly lit stores young shop-keepers with cotton head ties called out to the passers-by, and all along the streets red flags with signs of year-end sale fluttered in the wind. Women hurried along with small steps, tucking their hands into cotton-padded sleeves, the sound of their clogs cold under the dark December sky.

New Year's Day dawned gray and frozen, but toward afternoon it became a little warmer. Hazy sunshine began to peep through the clouds, and under the frozen surface of our pond, dim figures of carp flashed. Near and far, the rhythmical sound of battledore and shuttle-cock echoed, and different-colored kites were flying high up in the sky. In our dark entrance hall a varnished card tray was placed in front of a gold-leaf screen, and soon the stack of name cards brought by the silent callers grew high. Closer friends of the family stayed for a short visit and some *otoso* — spiced wine. Dressed in dark silk kimonos or in morning suits, they came and went, red-faced and merry, some even staggering a little as they left. And when my oldest brother returned in the evening from his calls, he too sounded very jolly.

"How was it?" Father asked at the dinner table.

"Oh, fine, Father," my brother answered a little vaguely.

"You made calls to all the homes I mentioned, of course?" asked Father. "You didn't forget any, I hope?"

"Well, to tell you the truth," said my brother, a little apologetically, "I lost the list you gave me. So I might have missed some of them."

"In that case," said Father matter-of-factly, "I will give you another one. Tomorrow will be the day for ladies' calls, so you can make up for the forgotten ones on the third."

My brother shifted uneasily on his sitting cushion. "I

thought I'd leave day after tomorrow . . ." he mumbled.

"Where to? School?"

"No — not exactly. I promised some friends to climb Hotaka with them before the term began."

"Climb — mountains?" Father sounded faintly surprised.

"Yes, Father."

"Well," said Father, and grew silent. When dinner was over, Father paused at the threshold. "Kazuo," he said. "Come to my room a little later. I wish to talk to you."

My brother frowned slightly. "About what, Father?" he asked. Mother looked at him anxiously, as if to say, "Don't speak to Father that way, Kazuo San," while my older brother and sisters excused themselves and left the room quietly. Father looked a little surprised at my brother's inquiry. "Nothing important," he said. "But if you are so inclined, we shall discuss it here." He stepped back into the room, and sat down on his cushion again. For a while he didn't say anything, but stared interestedly at the dwarfed plum tree in the corridor.

"What is it, Father?" my brother asked again.

Father turned his gaze on him, very thoughtfully, and began to pull at his mustache.

"Ah, yes. I wanted to ask you about your — mountain climbing."

"What about it, Father?"

"May I ask you why you must do it?"

"Well — I like it, Father," said my brother, a bit defensively.

"It hardly seems an occupation worthy of a gentleman to walk about aimlessly under a heavy load," observed Father.

"It isn't quite aimless — it trains the body."

"In that case why not train yourself with something like archery or judo? But do me the goodness of giving up mountain climbing."

"Why, Father?" There was a deep furrow between my brother's brows.

"Because it is dangerous."

"Not if you are careful."

"But there is a chance of one in ten thousand."

"People do not necessarily die in the mountains." My brother sounded exasperated. "Some people break their necks slipping on a staircase."

"The less reason for seeking an additional risk."

"Father does not understand," said my brother, and stared down a little sadly at the matted floor.

"Think of your responsibility," said Father very gently. "Remember that you are the eldest son. Your life is very important — not so much to yourself, but to our house. It is your duty to inherit our name and take care of our household after I pass away."

"There are the younger brothers," said my brother stubbornly.

"That may be so. But still, think of what Confucius said. 'One's body is inherited from one's parents. To take good care of it is the beginning of filial piety.'"

My brother kept silence.

"Think it over before you go."

"Won't you permit me to climb just this once, Father?" pleaded my brother.

"Why?"

"Because I promised my friends..."

"It is out of question to climb now."

"Why, Father?"

"It must be more dangerous with the snow."

"Then you won't permit me no matter what?" My brother's voice became quite angry.

"Calm yourself," said Father.

"Nothing will make me happier than to die in the mountains," said my brother determinedly.

"Do as you please," said Father, as if throwing a useless thing away. Mother, who kept silence all the time, one hand on the edge of the brazier, the other absently stirring the charcoal with a pair of copper chopsticks, raised her white, troubled face.

"Please, honorable husband," she said. "Let me talk to him. I am sure Kazuo will understand that your words are all for his own good, if given a little time..." Father looked away into the garden, at the trembling light on the lawn fading far into darkness, to the remaining patches of snow on a distant rock. "If he doesn't listen to all that I have said, let him do as he wants," he said wearily. "It's like chanting Sutra to a horse's ear..."

After Father left, my brother turned to Mother and said almost roughly, "Why is Father so strict with me, Mother? There is nothing I do that pleases him. I don't think he has ever liked me, even as a son."

Mother sighed. "That is because you are the eldest son, Kazuo. Father expects you to settle down and take over the family estate — and he believes discipline has to go with responsibilities..."

"Rice-cake maker's son must become a rice-cake maker, is that it, Mother?" My brother sounded bitter. "Father wants me to live exactly the way he does. I suppose he is happy — but I can never do it."

"Why, Kazuo San?" Mother sounded distressed.

"Look, Mother. I am not a scholar. I am not a retiring sort. I don't want to sit and live on hand-me-down property. I want to do something active."

"What, for instance?" asked Mother.

"Well — business, or continuing my research up in Hokkaido, or something. I want to try things and see what I like best first."

"You can do all that afterwards."

"After I grow old and moldy? That will be too late."

"Father does not object to what you really want to do — it's just your mountain climbing that he speaks of."

"It's all the same thing. If I retreat one step, he comes one step forward. We end up by doing what he wants anyway."

"Then you are going to continue climbing?"

"I suppose so, Mother," said my brother a little uneasily.

Mother looked down at the dying charcoal fire in the brazier, and gave a little sigh. "Is mountain climbing so important?" she said half to herself.

"There's something captivating about high mountains," said my brother. "I feel freer — I can breathe better."

Mother was still stirring the ashes with her copper fire tongs, vacantly making a neat little mound around the fire.

"You are young, Kazuo San," she said very quietly. "Too young."

Two days later, my oldest brother left for southern Honshu. Etsu helped pack his luggage, for she knew better than anyone how to prepare the young master for the bitterly cold weather of mountainous country. I watched her put pairs and pairs of thick knitted socks into the large rucksack, wrap coarse black bread in oiled paper with pieces of hard yellow cheese, and square bits of bitter chocolate, while my brother polished the alcohol lamp and examined his heavy leather boots with iron spiked heels.

"When would the young master return this time?" Etsu asked, looking up shyly. Her white cheeks were a little flushed from bending over her work.

"In about a week, I suppose," said my brother.

"I hope the young master will take good care of himself," said Etsu in a low voice.

"Thank you," said my brother. "I think with your careful preparation I shall survive at least this once."

"What an ill-omened thing to say," murmured Etsu, looking down. "May heaven forbid that anything should happen — ever..."

46. Rain and the Feast of the Stars

The day of the seven herbs passed, and the pine and tangerine decorations were taken away. The scroll of the seven gods of luck was replaced by one of eagle and the rising sun. The gold-leaf screen was folded away, and the household gradually went back to its quiet everyday life. But one morning, shortly after my brother left, Etsu didn't come to dress me as usual. I waited, wondering why and feeling lonesome in the cold nursery. When finally Etsu came, she was upset and absent-minded. She even forgot to tie my sash into a flower bow, but made it into a single knot as if I were a little boy, and not a girl at all.

I had my breakfast alone, and then was taken back to the nursery. "Where is Mother, Etsu?" I asked, climbing the stairs. "I have to go say good morning to her, you know." "The Mistress is busy this morning," said Etsu in her usual quiet voice. How funny, I thought. No matter how busy she was, I always went to say good morning to Mother. "Is Mother sick, Etsu?" I insisted. Etsu kept silence.

Why it was, I don't know, but I was a very bad child the rest of the morning. The picture book of the Little Bonze in the Wine Cup and the Tongue-Cut Sparrow did not interest me. I refused to be frightened by Etsu's story of the Snow Woman any more, and kept on grumbling until she left me and went downstairs. For a while I sat, looking out through the window at the dry, yellow lawn and the scattered maidenhair leaves, half regretting that I had been mean to Etsu. "Be good to Etsu, won't you?" My brother's words came back.

Perhaps I should go and find her. Perhaps I should say to Etsu I was sorry.

But on my way down I forgot about Etsu. Everyone seemed busy. The telephone bells were ringing. The house seemed like a different place, full of strange noises and whispers. And I began to feel uneasy once again — Perhaps, after all, Mother was sick. I had better go and find out. I had better go and say good morning to her. But she wasn't in her room.

"Hana, where is Mother?"

"The Mistress is having a guest. You must not disturb her now."

But I must go and find out, find out why everything was so different and strange this morning — and why I felt so left alone.

I tried to push open the heavy oak sliding door of our drawing room, but it wouldn't move. It was very cold in the corridor and my hands were freezing. I crouched down on the hard wooden floor and began to cry. The door opened, and Mother stood looking down at me, surprised. "Well — Reiko Chan. What is the matter with you? Isn't it a shame, in front of the visitors?" Mother sounded strict, but she wiped my tears away, took my hand, and led me into the drawing room. It was warm inside, for the fire burned cheerfully under the mantelpiece. Around the table sat several people, with pencils and pads in their hands, looking very serious.

"This is the youngest," said Mother. "Bow to the guests, Reiko."

My tears already dry, and feeling once again safe

and happy, I leaned against Mother's knee, looking at the strange visitors. For a while only the sound of the icicles melting in little drops sounded on the window sill.

"When did you get the news, Mrs. Hatsumi?" one of them broke the silence.

"We received it late last night," said Mother, sounding as if she was tired of repeating the same thing.

"Eldest son, wasn't he, Mrs. Hatsumi?"

"Yes."

"Can't we see the master of the house?"

"I am very sorry, but he is not feeling well today..."

I began playing with the tablecloth tassels, half listening to the conversation. Words floated by — meaningless words, floating and vanishing into the high dark ceiling. "Avalanche," "lost," "three others," "searching party," "the village inn"... Finally the flow of conversation slowed down and died away. After a pause one of them said, "We are very sorry about this, Mrs. Hatsumi. Of course there is still hope — for they aren't found yet. We will let you know as soon as any more news comes into the office."

"He went expecting danger," replied Mother calmly, with a little smile. "Even before he left, he said it would make him happy to die in the mountains..." I looked down at the tassels I was playing with, still leaning on Mother's knee. Then I noticed her hands on her lap, grasping a white handkerchief, holding on to it, trembling, twisting, as if they were in pain.

I looked up at her face, and she was still smiling.

"I am deeply obliged to you for your trouble." Mother

stood up, saw the guests to the door and bowed them out. I waited till she came back, stood near the window, and began arranging the flowers in a porcelain vase. "Mother," I called softly. "What is an avalanche?" "Ah, Reiko Chan. You are still here?" said Mother, vaguely. "Come, I will take you back to the nursery."

Etsu was sitting in the nursery, looking worried. As she saw us come in, she placed her hands on the floor and bowed. "I am very sorry, Honorable Mistress," she said. "I shouldn't have left Reiko Sama alone."

"That is all right," Mother said gently. "I am afraid it will be a little busy for all of you — for a while anyway. I am sorry about that."

"Honorable Mistress." Etsu, to my surprise, suddenly burst into tears. "I really don't know what to say ..."

"Etsu," said Mother, a little sternly. "Stop crying. The child is here."

"Mother," I said. "Please don't scold Etsu. I was very mean to her this morning. That is why she left me." Mother smiled again.

"I am not scolding Etsu at all. But you must be a good child anyway. Etsu, would you please tell all the maids that if any more reporters come, I am not feeling well today, and am *not* seeing any visitors." Then she was gone. Etsu wiped her tears with her kimono sleeve, and took up my socks again. "What story would Reiko Sama like to hear this afternoon?" said Etsu. I didn't know why, but she still looked very sad.

The only thing Father said, I learned later, when the news of my brother's death came, was "Foolish boy."

And those were the same words he spoke when the news came that my brother had been discovered — dug out miraculously from under deep snow. My brother was the only one alive out of four.

Several days later he came home with one arm in a sling, but otherwise looking quite as usual. This time he didn't go to say "I am back" to Father. He dined alone most of the time, and stayed in his room all day, smoking and reading.

For nearly a month he remained at home, till his arm was free of slings. Then he began to get ready to go back north. Once again Etsu was packing his suitcases, folding everything away with great care, singing a little song to herself in a small, silvery voice. She was singing of the Snow Woman who gives you milk and lures you far away into the dark and frozen hills... My brother was sitting in the sunny corridor, with his legs crossed, handling a pair of shiny brown skis.

"What are you doing?" I asked.

"Waxing."

"Are you going away again?"

"Ah-ha."

"To school?"

"No."

"Then where?"

"To the mountains," my brother replied briefly.

Cotton Cake
and a Bicycle

MY SISTER Michiko went to America when I was five years old. The purpose of her travel was to study at an Eastern college, although exactly what line of learning she pursued I have forgotten. It wasn't important, said Father, who believed in the educational value of traveling itself, and who also believed, unlike many of his contemporaries, that education was necessary even for girls.

On the day of Michiko's departure all my family, friends and acquaintances went to Yokohama to see her off, and I still remember how lovely she looked in her Japanese costume. She wore a pale, long-sleeved pink kimono with cherry blossoms — it being the season of cherry-blossoms — scattered all over it, and a navy blue serge overskirt, ankle length, all pleated — the typical attire of Japanese schoolgirls then. She spoke little English — correct, I suppose it was, but none too fluent. And she was too shy to throw, at the last moment, the balls of paper tapes from the first-class deck where she stood. So we were all very surprised when she finally mustered enough courage and asked a passing steward to throw us the tapes for her. The steward obliged. And we all held on to the ends of the many-colored tapes, while the ship sailed away slowly, amidst the cheers, fluttering handkerchiefs, and my mother's tears. Later, we had dinner at a Chinese restaurant, The White Moth, and came home.

During the ensuing two years my mother was always making packages and sending them off. Preserves, kimonos, sashes, fans — "I wonder what Michiko does with these things," Mother remarked once. "By this time she must have enough to set up a household over there..." What my sister did with those things remained a mystery, for she was not a very regular correspondent. But from all indications, my sister was spending her days at school busily and happily. And that was, I suppose, enough for Mother.

After two years my sister came home, without, as Mother had feared, establishing a household in America. But she came home with a mission. The mission of democratizing our household.

I shall never forget the moment when my sister came

trotting down the gangplank of the *Chichibu Maru*
that rainy September day. She was so completely
changed in appearance that I thought she must be a
stranger. Her hair, which she always had swept back
in a modest little bun, was now let loose, shortened and
waved. She wore a dark brown hat, beige one-piece
dress with beads shimmering down in the front, and
a pair of narrow-toed, very high-heeled shoes. In fact,
she appeared no different from the foreign ladies who
were coming down from the boat, before and after her.

"Well, Michiko San," said Mother, already in tears.
"I'm so glad you are back safe and sound."

"Why, of course, Mother," said my sister cheerfully.
"It was a wonderful trip. Too bad it ended so quickly."

I don't know whether Mother resented this remark.
Most probably she was too busy wiping her tears to
notice it.

So we came home, and had a grand dinner of welcome. My sister brought me a doll almost as big as
myself, and for my brother an air gun, and within the
next few days our household settled down to its normal
routine.

Or at least so my mother thought, for a while. Because the change came about gradually — very gradually
and imperceptibly. My sister's firm resolution of becom-
ing Americanized, and of Americanizing the rest of our
family, manifested itself in small things at first.

Several days after my sister's return her luggage
arrived. And on going through it my mother found no
trace of the things she had sent off while my sister was
still in America.

"What happened to all the kimonos you took there with you, Michiko San?" asked Mother, slightly alarmed. "Did you leave them there?"

"Oh, I gave most of them away, Mother," replied my sister nonchalantly. "People liked them so much, you know."

Mother was silent for a while. Then she said, with ever so light a tone of annoyance in her voice, "But Michiko San, what are you going to do just now? You will need your kimonos for visiting and parties — and it takes a little time to have them made all over again . . ."

"That's all right, Mother," said my sister, unperturbed. "I'm going to wear Western clothes from now on."

Mother raised her eyebrows, but didn't say a word. And from that day on, it was tacitly understood by my family that my sister was to wear Western clothes even when the rest of us didn't. It must have been a curious contrast, at some garden party or other, to see all the girls dressed in Japanese costume, looking dainty with their long sleeves and brocaded sashes, and my sister, a solitary figure in Western clothes, her face half concealed in what seemed like an inverted flower pot. Gradually she became known as the "Hatsumi family's second daughter who came back from America" — a label which marked her off from the other girls her age, and at the same time, I fear, somewhat lessened her marriage possibilities.

Mother may have been worried about it, but my sister seemed quite unconcerned. There were, as she said, more important things to think about than marriage.

More important things, such as the welfare of those around her. And since I was the youngest of the family, and the most pliable, my sister's attempts at revolutionizing the household were started on me. With great care she used to curl my straight black hair, tie huge flame-colored ribbons on top of my head, and encourage me to run around as much as possible in our formal garden, for she thought I was too quiet and spent too much time just sitting and reading.

Her experimentation went well so long as it did not bring me into contact with Mother. For although lenient in general as to how her children should be brought up, my mother did have decided views on certain things. The first clash, I remember, came on the day of *shi-chi-go-san*, a traditional feast for the children aged seven, five and three, when they are all dressed up and taken to temples and shrines, for no more particular reason than, as it seemed to me, to buy a bag of red and white candies and come back with a straw owl dangling from a bamboo rod clutched in our hands. At any rate, just as I was about to leave for a nearby shrine, all dressed up, my sister came out and saw me.

"Why, Mother," she said in a shocked voice. "Reiko has lipstick, rouge and powder on — and she looks horrible! At her age, Mother, it's ridiculous — it's not natural at all. In America, children her age *never* put make-up on..."

In vain Mother tried to point out the fact that it was just a custom, and quite an innocent one, and that most probably I would look, in my bright scarlet and gold

kimono, pale as a ghost without any rouge or lipstick on
— I was a very sickly child, and was always too pale and
thin to counterbalance the gorgeous coloring of Japanese
festive costume. My sister insisted on my washing my
face right away. Mother raised her eyebrows again, but
gave in, and I was taken to the bathroom and Etsu
wiped my face with a wet towel, looking quite gloomy
all the while.

I forget the rest of what happened on that day, except
that for some reason or other, people seemed to be
paying special attention to me as I went walking up the
stone pavement of the shrine with Etsu. Some went as
far as to turn around after I passed them, shaking their
heads as if to say they were sorry. Sorry about what, I
didn't know, unless my thinness made them think I was
there to pray for recovery from some childhood ailment.

Etsu of course didn't say anything — naturally, she
was just my nurse ... But for some reason or other, I had
a vague feeling that she didn't like my sister. It was all
the more incomprehensible because my sister took special care to be nice to all our servants. "We must treat
them like human beings," she used to say. "Not like —
not like — slaves or machines." Apparently Etsu didn't
like to be treated like a human being, and for that
matter neither did the rest of our maids. And I came to
that conclusion after observing several incidents.

There was, for instance, the question of my sister's
laundry. Ever since she had come home, my sister had
insisted on doing things for herself. Independence of
spirit, she called it. And although I suppose my sister's

insistence on washing and ironing her own clothes did relieve some of our maids' burdens, on the whole our domestic staff seemed to be a bit hurt by her behavior. "Of course," I heard Kiyo remarking to one of the under maids one day, "I don't suppose we could do the work as fine as the American people do, but still the young mistress could give us a try at it..."

Things became further complicated when my sister began insisting that the maids should not be kept up after certain hours, just because we happened to have some guests, who, unjustly unaware, or ignoring the convenience and human rights of our servants, chose to stay too long. "But Mother, it's inhuman," she was heard to say, "to keep them up, waiting all hours of the night for our handclaps — and they have to get up at six o'clock the next day..."

My mother agreed with her, as far as the sentiment went. But there was nothing she could do to solve the practical problem. So long as the guests chose to stay, Mother couldn't possibly suggest to them that they leave. And so long as the guests were there, it was unseemly for Mother or anyone else to stir about, producing tea-cups, refreshments and so on.

"The only thing I can think of, dear," said Mother resignedly, "is for them to take turns at staying up."

But that didn't work out either. For it ended up, usually, in the rest of the maids feeling sorry for the one whose turn it was to stay up, and all of them stayed up. "I couldn't go to sleep, Reiko Sama," said Etsu, quite logically, "while Kiyo San is staying up for I don't know how long. She has been here eight more years than I have. It would be quite improper for me to go to bed before she does..."

The next question was about the holidays. Servants, according to tradition, have two holidays a year. In summer, at the time of *Obon* — the days of the return of their ancestral spirits, and in winter, about the fifteenth of January. Now this seemed unspeakably cruel to my sister. "Why, in America, they have a day off every week, Mother. We should give them a holiday at least once a month."

Mother thought it was a fine idea, if the maids wanted it that way, and she would be glad to give them extra allowances and perhaps some kimono materials so they could go out more often... The change would have been welcomed by all, except for Mitsu, a pale, thin little girl who had been with us quite a long time, and whose parents lived not far away from us, right outside the city. It should have been nice for her, actually, for her home was so near — but Mitsu came from a family of eleven children, and had a stepmother who was a shrew, and a drunkard father. If she had a holiday, she would have had to go home. It would have been unthinkable for her not to; moreover, she would have had to spend most of her earnings in something to take home to her family, each time. Mother wasn't surprised when Mitsu came to her one day and hesitantly declined the privilege of having a holiday every month. She was in agonies, evidently, for she thought it was unpardonable to refuse the kindness of her patrons, and moreover to

seem ungrateful not only to her employer, but cold and
heartless to her own family.

"That's all right, Mitsu," said Mother consolingly.
"I was thinking you had better not go home just now too
often anyway. Instead of worrying about your family
too much, you should be getting things ready for yourself."

At that time I didn't know why Mitsu blushed so
deeply, and bowing, went away without a word. But
later I was to understand that my mother had just
received a proposal for Mitsu — quite a favorable one,
from an owner of a clog store — and was thinking of
arranging the match for her. So naturally Mother
thought it was better for Mitsu to save as much as she
could out of her salary and extra allowances, to enrich
the trousseau Mother was to give her.

There was a blow-up when my sister heard about it.
"Why, Mother! Arranging a match for Mitsu! *Arranging* a match — that's horrible. And I suppose she hasn't
even seen the man . . ."

"Mitsu doesn't seem to object to it, though," inter-
posed Mother mildly.

"Of course not," said my sister indignantly. "What
else could she do but to agree with you. You are her
employer, after all."

"What do you suggest I should do then?" asked
Mother. "Mitsu is nearly twenty-three, and she has to
settle herself sooner or later. It's getting late as it is —
unless she wants to stay with us for the rest of her
life . . ."

"Of course not," said my sister. "What I meant was that she should wait till someone who really cares for her comes along, and asks her to marry him. And not this go-between thing."

"Don't you think, Michiko San," said Mother quietly, "that perhaps the owner of the clog store has seen Mitsu several times — talked to her, and likes her — likes her enough to make her the mistress of his household, and mother of his children?"

"But what about Mitsu?" asked my sister, furious. "Doesn't she have a right to choose?"

"Of course, Michiko San," said Mother. "She can say 'no,' which she didn't."

That closed the argument, and within a few months Mitsu got married, looking till the last day as she always used to look, sad and thin and melancholy. After a year or so she had a fine boy baby, and came to show him to us, and ever after that, she always came to pay us a New Year visit, with boxes of candy or a basketful of fruits, looking happy and rosy, and much prettier.

Having been sadly disappointed in reforming our domestic condition, my sister turned her hopeful eyes to the outside world. Her education was complete, as far as schools went. Tea ceremony and flower arrangement, she said frankly, bored her. There was one thing left for her to do. She was determined to go to work.

The idea frightened Mother. "But Michiko San," she implored. "That kind of thing is simply not done — think of your friends — at least think of mine. No proper young girl works, unless she is an orphan or something. Why, you won't be able to get married..."

My sister was adamant. And every day the argument went on, till finally Mother gave in and my sister went to work, at an office of an Italian motorcar company situated in the Imperial Hotel. Shortly after she went to work, Mother invited her employers to our home for tea, and adopted them, so to speak, as our social friends. Mr. and Mrs. Viale arrived in a beautiful Fiat car, with several dozen lovely long-stemmed roses, and we became very good friends.

Everything, for the time being, went on smoothly. My sister liked her work, and after a while Mother became quite resigned. Once again, peace reigned in our household, till one day the storm broke loose. And it was, I think, really my fault.

Because I worshiped my sister in those days, I used to follow her around wherever I could. I would go up to her room, when she came home from work, finger all the curious and delightful foreign things that lay scattered about, ask questions, and in general make a nuisance of myself till she found some errand to send me off for a time. One day she asked me to go to the post office and mail a letter for her. I was delighted by the trust and confidence she showed me, and though never allowed to wander out of the house alone, set off immediately, and came home without getting lost on the way. I reported to my sister, and she fished a ten *sen* piece out of her purse and gave it to me. I was overcome with joy and surprise, for I had never had any money before that time. Although my older sisters and brothers received allowances after attaining the dignity and independence of commuting to and from school by themselves, most of the things we needed were procured for us. When, for instance, we wanted sweets outside of teatime, we asked Kiyo through our nurses and got them. If we needed something more important, Kiyo asked Mother and got it for us. And it was, of course, strictly forbidden for us to buy anything on our own, especially eatables.

Now, at that time, if there was anything that intrigued me in the way of food it was a cotton cake. Japanese cotton cakes are very ethereal things. They are like spun floss silk in pale rose and irridescent white, floating delicately around tiny wooden sticks, gossamer-thin and intangible — quite, so it seemed to me, out of this world. But to my grief cotton cakes were ruled out of my life by my strict upbringing. They were, as I was told, when I first expressed interest in them, what the *iyashii* children ate — *iyashii* meaning anything from low, common, indelicate and vulgar, to unmannerly, unrefined, uncouth and gluttonous — and many a time I had looked at those *iyashii* children with an envious side glance while they went skipping down the road with their beautiful cotton cakes.

Once, however, Mitsu, the little goodhearted Mitsu, took pity on my unexpressed desires, and on our way home from kindergarten bought me one. Bought me one, out of her own pocket, I recall with a tug at my heart. But alas, Mitsu too, like the rest of my family, was a prude. She insisted I wait to taste it till I reached home — at least till I was within the confines of our high stone wall. And that day happened to be a bit windy. Never have I hurried on my short little legs so much — running, practically all the way home, holding the cotton cake in my hand, and watching it dissolve gradually into the breeze with a feverish eye ... When we reached home I had nothing in my hand but a thin little stick, looking bare and forlorn. As I said, Japanese cotton cakes are ethereal things, ethereal and evanescent.

At any rate, when I received, so unexpectedly, the ten *sen* tip from my older sister, the first thing I thought of was a cotton cake. Now I could realize my dreams. Now I could get not only the pink cotton cake, but a white one as well, and perhaps eat them hidden behind the tall oak tree in the Kishimojin temple premises. I was growing very bold in my ideas. My sister's teaching was taking root, and I was acquiring a spirit of independence and enterprise.

The cotton cakes were sold in the temple premises, under one of the tall oak trees near the waterless well, by an old man with a flowing white beard. He sat behind an open, movable stall and spun out the delicate substance from an earthenware pot, stepping slowly on a wooden pedal down below.

My heart was beating very fast when I stood in front of the stall and placed the ten *sen* piece in silence on the side counter. The old man looked up and blinked. "How many do you want, little miss?" he asked in a quivering voice. I didn't know what to say, and kept silence. "One?" he asked. I shook my head. "Two?" I shook my head. "Three?" "Four?" "Five?" I didn't know how many cotton cakes I could get with ten *sen*, but thought it perhaps wise to come to a compromise, and nodded. The old man, without taking up the money, began spinning the floss silk around thin wooden sticks. One by one they were encircled by the ethereal pink and white substance, and after the fourth one I discovered I couldn't hold any more in my hands. It didn't occur to me to eat them; I was too fascinated by the spinning.

Just then I heard someone exclaim in a shocked tone right behind me, "My goodness, Reiko Sama! What on earth are you doing here? Are you alone?"

I turned around in a hurry, and found Miye San, an old-time seamstress of our home, standing behind me. She looked, somehow or other, triumphant, and for the moment I hated her.

"Why, you are alone, and buying *iyashii* cakes too," she exclaimed, gloating over her discovery. Miye San would have done anything not to miss the chance of getting into Mother's good graces. "We must go home at once," she said happily. The *iyashii* cakes were distributed among the *iyashii* children, and I was hustled home in disgrace.

A conference took place that evening, among Mother, Father, my sister and me. "But Mother, I didn't mean to do any harm," said my sister, almost in tears.

"What do you mean, 'no harm'?" asked Mother sternly. "When the time comes that Reiko needs an allowance, she will receive one. But in the meanwhile, I don't want her to have any strange notions. Why, running around on errands and receiving wages for it! How despicable! And moreover, to make her think she can go and buy whatever she wants! Why, Michiko San, would *you* be responsible if Reiko went and bought a rotten banana and became sick from it?"

"I didn't think of it that way," wailed my sister. "I asked her to do something for me, and I thought she was entitled to a reward. Why, in America, everyone works — even children and old people..."

"They do it here too," said Mother unperturbed. "Just go into any coal mine down South, and you will see children working. It's a pity, of course, and I hope something will be done about it."

"I didn't mean coal mines," said my sister. "Children work for pocket money, and nobody thinks anything of it — even well brought-up children."

Mother looked incredulous for a moment. "Well, I do think it is a shame that children have to work at all. It is of course fine to do so when necessary — but your father is not penniless, and I am not dying of tuberculosis. You can wait to train Reiko till such things happen."

My sister kept silence. I suppose she gave up at that point.

"At any rate," continued Mother, "I hope you will stop interfering with the way our life is run here at our home. I let you do whatever you wanted, for I thought you had to finish your American education here. But from now on, do forget about what you learned in America till you have a household of your own."

My sister still kept silence, looking down at the hem of the straw matting.

"And," continued Mother, a bit ironically, "be assured that I won't interfere with your way of running your life, when you get married and settle down."

All the while Father kept on sitting on his cushion, without saying anything.

Next morning I met Father walking in the garden.

"Well, well, Reiko," he said amiably. "How are things with you today?"

"Fine, Father," I said, ready to skip away.

"Nice weather, isn't it?" he said, still looking at me. "Yes, Father."

"By the way," he said absently, tugging at his mustache. "Do you want anything?"

"Do I want anything?" I must have sounded surprised. Father coughed. "I mean by that, is there anything you wish particularly to have?" he said, now seemingly intent on the growing vines of a morning glory.

I was surprised. He had never asked me a question of that sort before. Anything I wanted, or needed, was given to me by Mother, or more often by Kiyo. Father wasn't just the sort of person to ask for things. But the opportunity was there, and I wasn't going to let it pass. I thought for a while, and came out with an answer. "I want a little bicycle, Father," I said. My brother had one, and always insisted on carrying me behind him. But one day, going around the *sharinbai* tree, he upset the bicycle and since then it became a taboo for me to be his passenger. So I wanted to have one myself, although I knew Mother wouldn't like it.

Father thought also for a while, and then nodded his head. "Very well, you shall have it," he said.

"Thank you, Father," I said, skipping away.

A little blue bicycle arrived within a few days, and Father watched me try to ride it from the window of his study. I toppled over onto the lawn several times, then gave up. The little bicycle was put away into the godown and forgotten.

Years later, I came across it, rummaging for something else in the cellar. The bicycle was amazingly intact underneath the layer of dust, and looking at it I remembered, quite irrelevantly, the words once written by my father, "All changes must come from within. One cannot force anything, even good, on others." And those words, from a book banned by the wartime censorship, reminded me a little sadly how once his gift and advice went unheeded, by my sister, myself, and by the rest of the world.

At the
Mountains

EVERYTHING was the same at the sleepy little town
of Chino — the station with its black, weather-beaten
pillars, the slanting thatched roofs across the white, dusty
square, the burning orange of the pumpkin flowers that
clung to the hedge, hens clucking for food, and the
rows of dried persimmons hanging like wrinkled
Buddhist beads from the eaves. Everything — even the
silent group of children that stood staring, open-mouthed.

In front of the ticket office waited two taxis, looking
old and decrepit.

"Same cars," said Mother, a little unhappily. "I

wonder if they will make it up the hill to Tateshina?"

"They did last year," said Father. "No reason why they shouldn't this time. Nobody uses them except us anyway."

"You *are* quite optimistic, at times," said Mother.

Poor cars — they were aged, and suffered from asthma, but still they were our faithful friends that waited for us year after year at the quiet, forgotten mountain station of Chino.

So we piled into the taxis, said goodbye to the smiling station master and started on our way.

In the distance stood the Eight-Headed Mountain like a tall folding screen, deep blue against the turquoise sky. "Everything is the same," I thought, leaning on the hedge. There were the purple bell flowers nodding beside our gate, and at the back of our house the white birch grove stood, pale as usual, and silent. Just above my eyes on the rough-hewn gatepost hung our name plate, with Father's brushwriting almost wiped away by wind, snow and rain — "Cascade View."

Through the cryptomeria wicket and along the feathery bamboo brush I went around to the front garden. There was the stately camphor laurel, and under its shadow, tiny white dots of moon-viewing flowers. The cattails tickled my bare legs, and there was a scent of wild thyme in the air. Across the valley the cascade shone, like a silver-beaded screen hung on the green hillside.

Inside the house, tea was being served.

"Have another cup, Ojii San," my mother was saying. "Would you like some sweet bean paste?"

Ojii San, the aged proprietor of a nearby hot spring inn, slowly took up his fresh cup of tea. "Yes, Okusan," he said, "things have changed here, as you may notice."

"You mean the mines?" asked Father.

"Yes, Danna. Soon, this area will be crowded with people — with miners and speculators." There was a note of disapproval in his voice.

"It might bring some prosperity to the people here, though," said Father mildly.

"For how long?" inquired the old man, stuffing tobacco into a slender metal pipe. "They will come and blast the whole area, and when the copper is gone, they will go too." His voice sounded angry — angry but resigned. And he sat there, puffing at his pipe in silence.

"Ojii San," I said. "Where is Miyuki San? Why didn't he come with you?" Miyuki San, whose name meant deep snow, was his grandson whom I used to play with every summer.

The old man turned, and placed a large hand on my head. "Miyuki is gone to gather firewood, Reiko Sama. But tomorrow he will come to say 'Good day' to you."

Tomorrow — but tomorrow seemed a long way off...

"Isn't the picture finished yet? I am tired of sitting here — the sun burns on my hair..."

"Just a minute," said Miyuki San, looking up, and shading his eyes with one hand. He seemed quite serious, but as he watched me perched on a rock on the dry river bed, a smile appeared on his sun-browned cheeks. Underneath a coarse wadded-cloth jacket Miyuki San looked thin, but his eyes, dark and sensitive, had a curious coolness under the burning sun.

He glanced down at his sketchbook, and his face became serious again. "You move too much, Reiko Sama," he said a little sadly. "Perhaps we will finish it some other time..."

"Let me see." I ran up, and leaning on his shoulder, gazed down at the open page. A strange face looked up at me — almond-shaped eyes under short, straight bangs, a mouth slightly drooping at one corner.

"Is this me?" I asked, awed.

Miyuki San nodded. "It isn't good. I mean, it's not finished yet. We'll do it some other time." He closed the sketchbook with a snap. "Some other time when the sun is not so hot..."

The warm, yellow sun fell like a blanket over and around us. It fell on the dusky-pink wood berries, shining soft and moist on the dry riverbank. It fell on the reeds, the ferns, and the cluster of delicate pale green goose-grass. Bees hummed around the wild pomegranate tree, and the catch-fly violets yawned in the shade, slowly curling and uncurling their fingers, hideously grinning.

"What are you thinking about, Miyuki San?"

"I don't know," said Miyuki San, a little blankly. He

sat, hands clasped around his knees, gazing at the swirling, dark green water at our feet. "I was wondering — where this river goes."

"It goes down to the sea, doesn't it?"

Miyuki San didn't say anything, but began pulling at the long, bladelike reeds and tearing them one by one to tiny shreds. After a while he spoke again. "I wonder how long it takes, crossing those mountains."

I looked up. The Eight-Headed Mountain stood far away, towering above the horizon, misty blue and forbidding. "You can't cross those hills ... Mother said there weren't any roads."

"Perhaps — that's why I was thinking I can go down along the river."

"But you will be very tired before you get to Chino."

"That doesn't matter," said Miyuki San. "I won't get tired."

"Why do you want to go away? Don't you like it here?"

"It's not that," said Miyuki San. "I want to go to a big city because I want to keep on studying."

"Study?"

"Yes — study painting."

"And then?"

"And then ..." he faltered, and began biting a blade of reed between his strong white teeth. "You see," he said slowly, "it really doesn't matter — what happens, so long as I can keep on doing what I honestly want to do ..."

"Oh."

"And then — perhaps someday I can find my mother to..."

His mother — I had never heard him speak of his mother. I didn't even know that he had one.

"She shouldn't have gone," said the wagtail, hopping on the riverbank. "She shouldn't have gone," said the water, splashing over the rocks.

"Oh well." Miyuki San shrugged his shoulders. He gathered a handful of pebbles from the river bed, and began throwing them into the deep.

"Don't do that — Hana said there is a spirit living down there. You shouldn't offend him, or he will do you harm..."

Miyuki San laughed. "That's silly, Reiko Sama. You mustn't believe in such things..." But he threw the rest of the pebbles away and stood up. "It's getting late, Reiko Sama. The crows are going home, and the sixth bell of the mountain temple will be ringing soon. Your mother must be wondering where we are."

"*Ka-ka-ka,*" the ugly black birds crowed in the pale blue evening sky. Through the brushes and up the hill we went, into the plateau dotted with purple thistle flowers and the blond eulalia waving in the slanting sun. The temple bell began to echo in the faraway hills, and above, the clouds glowed, madder-red against the western sky. Tomorrow would be another fine day...

One by one the black and white stones filled up the square *go*-board. Two figures, one mustached, in black silk kimono, and the other round-shouldered underneath a blue working jacket, sat facing each other on the matted floor. In the corner of the room, on an oblong brazier, a copper teakettle murmured, and next to it the *oshosan*, a priest from the mountain temple sat holding a string of acorn beads under his sleeve. Sunshine, coming in through the open corridor, fell obliquely on the gnarled water-oak pillar — a pillar, I thought, very much like the old innkeeper himself, dark and solid and worn with age. Everything was old at the hot spring inn — old and weather-beaten. The high, dark, soot-coated ceiling, massive rafters, even the big tortoise-shell cat that curled up in the corridor, dozing.

"By the way, Ojii San." Father's remark fell like a pebble into the deep silence. "Your grandson seems to have grown quite a bit since last summer."

Slowly the old innkeeper looked up from the go-board. "Yes, Danna. On your account Miyuki is getting to be quite a good help."

"How old is he?"

"Thirteen."

"What do you intend him to do in the future?" asked Father.

"What will I make him do?" the old man sounded surprised. "Why of course, he will take over this inn after I pass away."

"The boy seems to be inclined otherwise," said Father gently.

"Otherwise?" asked the old man, looking puzzled.

"I understand he wants to keep on studying — painting, that is," explained Father.

The old man shook his head and laughed. "Painting indeed! What has got into his head — the boy must be crazy."

"He may have talent," said Father. Then he added, half to himself, "Even if he has to be disappointed, why not let him try first?"

But the old man shook his head again. "Why, we don't even have enough money to send him to middle school."

"We might be able to arrange that," said Father, smiling slightly.

The old innkeeper straightened himself. "Thank you, Danna. I know you mean well, and I know the boy wants to draw. But you see —" He hesitated. "You see, my daughter-in-law was a city woman. She left us after our son died. It couldn't be helped. She was a woman, and she was young. But the boy should remain — with the house. And I don't want the village folk to say 'Look, it's in the blood. Now her *son* goes away too.'" His voice faltered, and he looked out of the corridor at the mountainside, at the flowing river across the garden. "Why," he murmured, "my father's father lived here among those hills and was content..."

The copper teakettle sizzled in the shadow. In the patch of the lingering sun the tortoise-shell cat stood up and raised its back, purring.

"I too," said the bonze, breaking his silence, "had wished to see the world when I was young. And having finished my apprenticeship at the holy mountain of Koya, I walked from one hallowed ground to another, begging my way. But now, whether being in these far-away mountains or being in a large city, it does not seem to make any difference. Young people, however, must have their own feelings about such matters," said the bonze, gently smiling.

Our shadows lay long and thin in front of us, trembling on the stony mountain road. From time to time huge black butterflies flitted across our path, and above, clouds of dragonflies skimmed through the air, shining rainbow-colored in the last rays of the sun.

"Father, isn't Miyuki San coming with us to Tokyo?"

"No." He sounded surprised. "Were you listening?"

"Why isn't he coming back with us, Father?"

"Because Ojii San doesn't want him to."

"Why doesn't Ojii San want him to?"

"Because —" Father paused, as if trying to look for words. "Because he is an old man, and doesn't like changes."

"Not even for a visit?"

"I don't think so."

"Why?"

"Because." Again Father was silent for a little while. "Country people do not trust big cities. Ojii San is afraid Miyuki will never come back once he is gone."

"Wouldn't he?"

"I don't know."

Purple mist began to rise from the valley, and far away a string of pale blue smoke wavered up into the jasper-colored sky. The tiny, dainty leaves of the *nemu* tree were closing one by one in the falling shadow, and over our heads a row of wild geese flew by, crying in the violet blue dusk.

The honey looked like pure topaz and had a faint fragrance of jonquils. It lay on my tongue like dew, heavy, sweet and clinging.

"Who made it, Miyuki San?"

"Farmers down in the village," said Miyuki San. We were sitting on the back porch, facing the white birch grove. The air was cool and the ground was wet with dew. From time to time sandflies went by, faintly buzzing. Early that morning Mother sent Miyuki San down to the village, and he came back with a big *sake* bottle full of clear, citrine-colored honey.

"I must go and give it to your mother," said Miyuki San, but he didn't move.

"I will," I said. "But there's no hurry..."

Miyuki San sat, tracing something on the ground with a piece of twig. A line to the right, a line to the left, then a straight line underneath — after a while a range of mountains appeared, with a river circling its bottom, flowing away somewhere out of sight.

"I saw a car today down in the village," said Miyuki San, throwing the twig away.

"A car?"

"A motorcar," he explained a little shortly. "It wasn't a truck, and it wasn't at all like the old taxis at Chino.

It was black and shiny, and there were some city people with strange machines. People said they came to look at the mine."

"Did you talk to them?"

"No, but I was wondering where the car came from. I wanted so much to ask them — if they would give me a ride."

"Ride where?"

"Anywhere — out of these hills, as far as they would take me."

"Ojii San wouldn't like it, Miyuki San."

"I know."

For a while we sat silent. A cloud went over the grove, casting a chilly shadow. Somewhere in the sky, a sound of thunder echoed. "Rain, rain, rain," noisy, chatterbox shrikes sang in the wood.

"Rainstorm is coming," called Father, coming through the gate in a hurry. "You had better go in before it gets too cold." Then he noticed Miyuki San and stopped. "Ah — Miyuki, I must talk to you." Father stood there, pulling at his mustache, forgetting about the coming storm. "About the picture you drew — of Reiko. I would like to buy it. That is, if you don't mind receiving — er — money," he added politely.

Miyuki San flushed. "I don't have any use for money," he said, stammering. "I drew it because I wanted to."

Father coughed. "What I thought was, Miyuki, perhaps you could buy yourself such things as drawing paper and crayons. But of course, if you would rather have them sent over from Tokyo..."

Miyuki San was thinking, his head bent down, staring at the ground. Then he said, raising his eyes and looking straight at Father, "Thank you, Danna Sama. I will receive the money then."

Father looked relieved. "Then you better come in too," he said, opening the paneled porch door.

Ash-colored cloud began to swirl in the darkening sky. At the back of our house the birch trees fluttered, and with the first gush of wind came the drops of rain, heavy and cold, hitting our windowpanes like tiny balloons exploding.

It rained for a day and a night, and the sky became blue again. The whole range of mountains shone bright green under the sun, and in our garden drops of water glistened on the round mulberry leaves. But the river rose, muddy and roaring, pushing through the ravine in an eddying torrent, tossing rocks and carrying along huge branches down into the valley.

"It will take days," said Mother, "for the water to recede. You mustn't go out for a while, Reiko. Some of the roads may be washed away."

Late in the morning the old innkeeper came hurrying into our garden. "Where is Danna?" he asked breathlessly. "I must see him at once." He was in such a hurry that he even forgot to say good day.

"What is the matter, Ojii San?" Father asked. "A fire?"

"Miyuki is gone," said the old man, his eyes blinking.

"We didn't worry at first, thinking he must have gone to see about our field. But then we found this note in the family shrine. I am sorry to trouble you, Danna, but would you please read it for me?" The piece of white paper trembled in his hand.

Father put on his glasses and began slowly reading. "Ojii San," it said. "I am very sorry to leave like this, so suddenly. It is not that I have forgotten what the teacher at school and the *oshosan* told me — that the debt of gratitude to one's parents is deeper than the sea, and higher than the mountains. But please do not be angry with me. Someday I will come back to resume my duties as a son. Please tell Obaa San not to worry, for I shall be all right."

"If only I hadn't scolded him," said the old man, drooping.

"What did you say to him, Ojii San?" asked my father.

"I said to stop drawing if it gives him such a preposterous idea as going to a city. Perhaps I spoke too harshly. But I thought it was best for him..." Big drops of tears came rolling down from his eyes, tracing a streak on his furrowed, sunburnt cheeks. And he stood there in our garden, wiping them away with his hard, wrinkled fists.

"Everyone knows him in the village." Mother tried to console him. "Somebody will stop him on the way."

"Did you notify the policeman?" asked Father.

"I am on my way," said the old man, "now that I know what the letter says..." He bowed, and went out of our gate. The sun shone, coldly, brightly on his bent shoulders as he went with short, hurried steps down the hill.

"Mother, where did Miyuki San go?"

"I don't know."

"Will he come back soon, Mother?"

"I don't know — now go and play with Hana."

But I couldn't find Hana. So I put on my shoes and went outside, alone. A breeze swept over the eulalia-covered field like a prolonged sigh. Beside our gate a clear little stream ran down in the newly made gully, and the bamboo-leaf boat I set sailing went dancing, soon out of sight. A huge white cloud shone on the mountain shoulder, white and dazzling and lonely. And as I watched, the outer edge of the cloud became blurred in my tears.

"What is the matter?" said Father, coming up to the gate. "Has your brother been teasing you again?"

"No, Father, it isn't that . . ."

The cloud dissolved and floated away into the blue, and the tears tasted bitter in my mouth.

"Let's go inside the house, Reiko. I will tell you the story of the bamboo bear I once met in the mountains . . ."

How many times had I heard that story — it was the only one Father knew. But I didn't care — it was a story.

"One day, as I was walking down the hill, that hill near the Misty Cascade . . ."

83. At the Mountains

The room was quiet, and far below, beyond the hedge and the shrubbery, in the deep ravine the river sounded, loud and mournful, hurrying down, down to the sea. And on my father's knee I went to sleep, listening to his tale of the bamboo bear.

Across the valley, the fresh red-brown crevice looked like a raw scar on the green hillside. I sat on a rock, my toes in the pure, crystal cool water, feeling the warm sunshine on my back. Behind me in the garden Ojii San's hatchet sounded, rhythmical and monotonous.

"Would you like a cup of tea?" The old woman came out to the corridor, holding a kettle and a small round tray.

The old man stopped working and sat down on the chopping block, wiping his forehead with his sleeve. "Would you be coming back next summer?" he asked, taking up his teacup.

"I don't know," I said.

"You may not come back at that," said Ojii San. "They have begun working on the mine already, I hear. And you know how your father likes quiet..."

The yellow, coarse-leafed tea steamed up in the tiny china cup, and the mugwort dumpling looked surprisingly fresh and green, tasting of early spring and young leaves.

"It will be lonesome with all of you gone," said Obaa San, placing the tray in the corridor. "And now, just the two of us..." Streaks of silver shone in her neatly coiled hair as she bent down to pour some more tea.

She was thinking, I felt, of the little family shrine in the corner of their kitchen, where there was a tablet, a newly made white tablet with a long Buddhist name I couldn't read.

"*Baa San ya*," said the old man, taking up another piece of mugwort dumpling. "It's no use repeating — there are things that can't be helped." But the piece of dumpling trembled in his hand too.

The river went rushing and singing over the rocks, indifferently. A kingfisher flew across the water, flashing jade-green in the sun.

"If only I can keep on doing what I honestly want to do..." Life was like the river. It kept on moving, carrying things away, out of one's reach.

"Thank heaven," said Mother, "the packing is done." She stood in the middle of the room, looking happily over the piles of trunks and suitcases.

"The truck is late," said Hana, kneeling down to tighten the rope of a quilt case.

"A little," Mother answered. "But it doesn't matter so much what time we get home — it's not like coming up here..."

Outside the hills lay shimmering in the sun, and in our garden burning red amaranth nodded beside the hedge. *Kana-kana-kana*. A cicada sang its early evening song in the woods. Somewhere far, the sound of an explosion echoed.

There was a scuffling sound in the front garden, and

through the crytomeria wicket my sister came running, laughing as she went by into the white birch grove. My brother came running after her, brushed past me, and disappeared.

"That's not fair — that's half mine..." His voice trailed off into the trees.

I went slowly up the hill to our gate, picking at the curling brake ferns. The reeds hung their heads heavily on the ground. The tiger lilies were gone, and instead, a mass of purple *kuzu* flowers lay scattered on the field. Tall, thin passanias nodded and wavered above my head, and the larch trees kept shedding their leaves gently in the breeze.

Over the hills and the valleys came an echo of the temple bell. "All human deeds are of no avail: all living beings come to an inevitable end..."

The maple leaves were already turning. Soon the whole range of mountains would be covered with scarlet and gold. *Kana-kana-kana.* The voice of the cicada sounded again, clear and trembling. Clouds were racing in the high, blue sky. There was autumn in the sound of the wind.

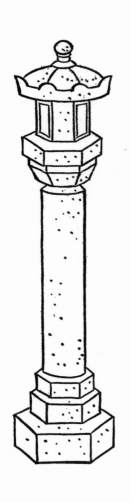

Between Heaven
and Paradise

It started long ago, my wandering pilgrimage between Heaven and Paradise. Because I was small, and there were conflicting influences around me, it was difficult to decide which one I should choose...Mother said I was to go to heaven—eventually, that is, and if I were a very good child. Bahya, my old nurse, thought otherwise. Not that she would have contradicted Mother in any way—oh, Bahya would never have done that. Instead she told me how beautiful *her* paradise was, with silver sands and crystal pagodas, iris shimmering in the perpetual sun, and coral berries, so delicate, as if hand-carved...

So my loyalty was divided, and even now — even now I feel guilty, finding myself in the chapel dreaming of heaven with flowering lotus blossoms and rainbow-colored *mandalas*. Then I become at a loss where to place the little cherubs, harps and shining white clouds, and harmonize them with the rest of my oriental paradise...

But had I really a choice between the two? Not according to Mother. For I was, like my brothers and sisters, a born Catholic.

"A new catechism class begins at the Cathedral next week," said Mother to Father one day. "I think we'll have to send Reiko — Father Flaujacque mentioned it to me specially the other day."

Father sounded reluctant at first. "Why not wait till she goes to school?" he asked. "The child is small and delicate. What is a year or two delay? She can receive her First Communion at the Sacred Heart Convent."

"Forgive me for returning your words," said Mother. "But you know Father Flaujacque..."

"I know him. What of it?"

"You know how particular he is about such matters ...I suppose we *could* trouble the Archbishop. But considering the other members of the church, if *we* made exception in case of *our* children..."

"I see," said Father, with a little note of annoyance.

So one fine Saturday afternoon I left home for the Cathedral, dressed in a red velvet frock and with a ribbon in my hair. Jiiya, our old manservant, accompanied me. For a while we walked on in silence through the quiet streets. The day was soft and warm, and there was a scent of plum blossoms in the air. Pale pink and delicate they were, cascading over the hedges like a ghost of early spring.

"Jiiya." I wanted to stop and gather the fallen petals that lay scattered like fragments of snow — they would look so pretty in a cup of green tea. But Jiiya kept on walking as if he hadn't heard. He looked determined, somehow, pattering along in his hemp-leaf sandals, with a long bamboo pipe jutting out from his mouth. So I gave up, and skipping, caught up with him.

Finally, when the pointed spire of the Cathedral came into view, I began to feel uneasy.

"Jiiya," I said, and tugged at his hand. "Do you think there will be many children there?"

My old manservant stopped and took out the bamboo pipe from his mouth.

"Certainly," he said, with a slight smile underneath his wrinkled eyelids. "Little Mistress will make many friends to play with from now on."

"I don't know," I said, feeling more reluctant as I thought about it. "I don't think I want to play with many friends — I'd rather stay at home and play with Etsu."

"Little Mistress will change her mind when she sees so many young ladies of her age," said Jiiya, patting my head.

"I don't know," I said. Suddenly, I don't know why, I was frightened...

The room was cold and dark and bare. Children sat on rows of narrow hard wooden benches, their hands folded, without stirring. They were healthy-looking children, brown and barefooted, dressed in simple, somber-colored kimonos. At the head of the rows of benches stood Father Flaujacque, a formidable figure in his black cassock.

"*Tiens,*" he boomed, "today, we are to study the Ten Commandments, am I correct?" Then, having looked around the room, he pulled up a chair and subsided. "Recite the first five, Taro."

One by one the children stood up and answered Father Flaujacque's question, while he sat nodding his head, stroking his long, shiny red beard, and occasionally glaring at the faltering children with his pale blue eyes. Once he made a little boy stand in the corner, for apparently he hadn't done his homework. I was getting more and more frightened. What if he asked *me* a question, and I couldn't answer it, I wondered. Would I have to stand in the corner too? My feet were cold and numb, and the roaring cough of Father Flaujacque almost started me crying. Sitting on the hard uncomfortable bench, with both hands on my lap, I thought of my quiet nursery with warm sunshine and the green leaves of crape myrtle looking in from the window, my damask-clad dolls and the steaming sweet bean gruel that Etsu made for me.

After the catechism we had thirty minutes of recreation before the rosary hour, and were all herded out to the playground. I stood alone at the entrance of the meetinghouse, leaning against the stone pillar, not knowing what to do. A group of girls came up, hand in hand.

"Can you play *shagami-oni?*" one of them asked.

"No," I said, feeling lost. "But I'd like to."

It was a strange game — that *shagami-oni*. You had to run around and catch someone before she crouched down on the ground and cried "Safe." Soon I became tired of running back and forth, trying to get another girl to take my place as *oni* — the demon. No matter how much I tried, how fast I ran, I couldn't catch anyone. Finally I gave up. "I can't run any more," I said, panting.

"Dressed-up sissy," sang the girls. "She can't even run." Soon the boys joined the chorus, and one of them pulled my ribbon away, skipping and laughing.

I turned my back to the crowd and ran to the gate, looking for Jiiya. I couldn't cry in front of those children, I thought. I shouldn't cry in front of anyone. But when I saw Jiiya sitting by the gate, peacefully puffing at his slender bamboo pipe, I couldn't hold back my tears any longer.

"What happened, Reiko Sama?" he asked. "Did someone do any mischief?"

"They said my dress was funny," I sobbed. "And they said I was stuck-up."

"Who said such things? I will see that my Little Mistress is not insulted," said Jiiya angrily.

"No, Jiiya," I said, wiping my tears. "It's all right. I'll ask Mother and she'll never make me come again."

"That is the best thing to do," agreed Jiiya. "We will never come here again."

But Mother, to my surprise, said I must keep on going.

"What are you going to do when you go to school,

Reiko?" she asked. "There will be many more girls then.
And it's about time you learned how to play with children your own age."

"But I don't want to play with any children," I
pleaded. "Please, Mother, I will learn all the catechism
by heart — if you will only let me stay home."

Mother looked at me in silence, then said more gently,
"I don't want you to do what you really don't wish to
do, Reiko Chan. But do understand — we have to obey
the Reverend Fathers in whatever they say. If Father
Flaujacque thinks all the children in his parish should
come to the church and be properly educated in their
religion, we must do as he tells us. So try a little longer
— you will get used to it after a while."

But I never got used to my life at the church, although
I didn't speak about it to Mother again. Soon the children got tired of teasing me, but I never made friends
among them. They dressed differently. They behaved
differently. And the way they spoke sounded strange to
my ears, accustomed to the slow, ceremonious speech
used at home. Week after week I went to catechism class
with Jiiya, walking slowly, ever so slowly, till he pulled
my hand and said, "Do let us hurry, Little Mistress. I
know you dislike to go. But Jiiya will be scolded if we
come too late."

Week after week dragged along. Saturdays and
Sundays — catechism, choir practice, Rosary, stations of
the Cross, confessions for the older children, Benediction... "What are the six commandments of the
Church?" "What is a dogma?" "What are the five
joyous mysteries of the Rosary?" What were they — I

wasn't listening anymore. It was much more pleasant to think of something else — about the little angels, for instance, that were in my holy picture card. "We each of us have a guardian angel," said Father Flaujacque, "that accompanies and protects us wherever we go." But they can't be here, I thought. It's too dark and gloomy and cold — surely they must be waiting outside. I pictured our guardian angels standing around in the sun, in their long white frocks, some yawning, some dusting their shiny wings. They were blessed people, with haloes and blue eyes and curly golden hair, but the most important thing was that they were free — they didn't have to come to the church every week and listen to boring lectures. They didn't have to be frightened and scolded, and bring written excuses from their mothers the time after they were absent — for they lived in a city of jade and pure gold, and could go back there whenever they wanted to.

Why were there so many things that were sins in the Catholic Church? And why were there so many things that were sins if you didn't do them? Bahya went to her temple only twice a year — and yet nobody scolded her. It seemed so much easier to be a good Buddhist than a Catholic. Or was it a sin in itself to entertain such thoughts? It must have been — for I was punished, and the God of Jehovah is a jealous God...

It was a beautiful Sunday in early June, when rain-washed leaves shone bright green in the sun, and the air was fresh and crisp. Father Flaujacque gathered all the parish children before the Mass began. *"Tiens,"* he said, stroking his beard. "You have come, I hope, well prepared to receive the Holy Communion today. As I told you last Saturday, Corpus Christi is a special celebration of the Holy Eucharist. Every one of you should realize the significance and the privilege of being allowed to partake in this divine sacrament. Especially the First Communion class of this year..."

What shall I do? I thought in panic. Early that morning, I had a piece of chocolate, not only forgetting that it was Sunday, but also not knowing that it was such an important one. What if I raised my hand and told him I couldn't receive Communion because I had a piece of chocolate that morning? No—I couldn't possibly do that. The best thing is just not to go...

The altar was decorated with white carnations and pale pink gladioli. There were more candles than usual, and the floor was covered with thick red carpet. The Archbishop and his assistants, dressed in gold-encrusted robes, came slowly in through the center aisle. The Mass began, and all during the first half of it I worried about what to do. What would Father Flaujacque say if I didn't go to Communion? If I stayed behind alone? He might come up and ask me what was the matter. Then what would happen?

"Agnus Dei, qui tollis peccata mundi," sang the choir, solemn and forbidding. *"Agnus Dei, qui tollis peccata mundi: miserere nobis..."* If I went, I thought, that will be the end. I shall commit a mortal sin—a sin of sacrilege, which was worse than dying...

"Domine, non sum dignus," said the acolyte, striking his breast. The candles flickered on his brocaded robe as he bent down in front of the altar. *"Domine non sum dignus..."* Someone touched my shoulder. I turned my head. It was Mrs. Makino, the catechist. "Don't be absent-minded," she whispered. "It's Communion now." "I..." I opened my mouth to say something, but Mrs. Makino interrupted me. "Sh — hurry, hurry. The other children are about all gone." I turned around, looking desperately for Mother. But the side pews were too dark, and it was difficult to distinguish one veiled figure from another. At the back entrance stood Father Flaujacque, watching. Mechanically I stood up, joined the double row of children and went up to the altar rail.

They once told me that if an unworthy communicant approached the altar rail, the Holy Eucharist would float up in the air, away from the mouth of the sinner. In all earnestness, I expected this to happen. But unfortunately it didn't. Instead, I felt a sharp little pain inside as I received the Host. And I knew, as I came back to my seat on the matted floor, that the pain was not of fright but of despair.

"What happened to Reiko? She looks like a little old woman nowadays," said Mother. "Look at the wrinkle on her brows — one would think she had something to worry about."

It might have been true, what people said. That I was too young to worry about things. But Bahya, if she were there, would have worried with me. She would have noticed that my cheeks were paler, that I was quieter than usual, and that I ate less. Bahya would have gone to pray at the local shrine, and in the evenings would have knitted a crimson bib — an offering to the stone statue of Gizo, the guardian deity of children.

But Bahya was no longer there, and the little round-headed statue stood half buried in the roadside brush, wearing faded bibs and with shriveled flowers at his feet — tribute of once distressed mothers who have gone away and forgotten.

And I kept my worries to myself.

Underneath the shadow of a high Gothic vault, a light keeps on burning — a little red light that flickers, but never goes out. Behind it stands the altar, cold and immaculate, surrounded by a host of angels in blue and white, their silent profiles half buried in the gloom. Sunshine, rainbow-colored and shimmering, falls from the tall stained-glass window and stretches on the matted floor. The huge Cathedral is deserted.

"Hail Mary, full of grace..." An orange-colored light stops on my tiny hands and trembles. A light from the yellow robe of Mary Magdalen kneeling at the foot of the cross in the stained-glass window.

"Hail Mary, full of grace. The Lord is with Thee..." My prayers escape like a sigh, prolonged and faltering.

What is the use of praying? For a soul that has committed a mortal sin cannot pray and be heard — isn't that what Father Flaujacque said? And he must know...

At the right-hand side stands Our Lady, who has an

altar all her own. And I address my prayers to her. Perhaps you can help me...But she keeps on smiling, sweetly, a little sadly, without saying anything. Her robe of white and gold glistens in the dark, and the serpent underneath her feet twists in the shifting light, as if in eternal agony.

What is the use? Since my prayers will never be heard...I stand up, and crossing myself, steal out of the cathedral like a guilty shadow, into the sunshine...

Across the courtyard children played, forming a circle and going around, singing. I walked down the stone steps and went past them, in silence. Past the meetinghouse and the kindergarten, past the rectory and then — I almost bump into someone.

"Où allez-vous, mademoiselle?"

I look up in surprise. A tall person stands in front of me — Archbishop Chambon in his scarlet robe and heavy gold chain of office, with his snow-white hair, and kind, blue, saintly eyes. "Où allez-vous, Mademoiselle Reiko?" he asks again, very courteously.

"I — don't know," I stammer, feeling shy. I really don't know where I am going. Home, perhaps — not that it matters...

The Archbishop stands there, looking down at me. "And how is your family, mademoiselle?"

"Fine, thank you, Monseigneur."

There is something soft, something warm in his smile. Just like a grandfather's, I think, although I have never seen mine.

"Perhaps you would like to see my flower garden?"

suggests the Archbishop, fingering his golden chain. I nod, remembering the last time he was at my home. He said he liked gardening because he was "a farmer from Normandy..."

"Come." The Archbishop takes my hand, and begins walking back toward his big stone residence.

The flower garden is small, but it is quiet. Patches of ground, partitioned off by bricks, lie next to each other along the ivy-hung wall. Flowers, scarlet, yellow, and white, lift their heads in the sun, turning to all directions and gently swaying.

"Those are zinnias, and this is delphinium. And there," says the Archbishop, pointing toward a glass-covered dome, "is my conservatory."

The conservatory stands half above the ground, half below. A speck of sunshine stops on its dusty window-pane and sparkles. I peep in, but there are no flowers.

"No flowers — they are all sleeping now," says the Archbishop, looking in too. "Or perhaps they have all gone to heaven..." He tips his head, and glances up toward the sky, smiling. "But here — just a minute." He steps down lightly and stooping, goes in through the wood-framed archway. From one of the pots in the corner he picks up a big, purple, curly plant and hands it to me. It doesn't look like a vegetable, but neither does it look like a flower.

"What is it, Your Excellency?"

"It is called a leaf peony," says the Archbishop. "It is half flower, and half cabbage. And it grows only in Japan."

"Oh..." For its size, the flower cabbage feels light in my hands — light and dewy, and softly trembling.

"*Merci, Monseigneur.*"

"*Du tout, mademoiselle.*"

"*Au revoir, Monseigneur.*"

"*Au revoir, mademoiselle.*"

Very gradually the sun was sinking toward the horizon. Along the streets, in the lengthening shadow of the eaves, swallows flitted. "What would he say, if he knew?" I wondered, walking home, alone. "If he knew — he would never smile at me again. And probably he would never give me another flower cabbage — a flower cabbage that didn't go to heaven with the rest..."

I found Jiiya sitting in the back yard, mending a pair of clogs underneath a mulberry tree.

"Plant this for me, will you, Jiiya?" He looked up with a smile on his wrinkled face as I handed him the flower cabbage.

"The best thing to do, Little Mistress, is to put it in water in a flat vase. But sit down here, and Jiiya will gather some raspberries for you," he said, taking off his blue cotton head tie and spreading it out on a stone for me.

"I don't want any raspberries, Jiiya," I said, sitting down wearily. "I don't want anything."

Jiiya looked at me curiously with his sunken eyes. "You *are* sick then, Little Mistress. I heard the maids talking..."

"No, I'm not sick, really."

"But Little Mistress does not sing and skip around any more as she used to do."

"I have something to — worry about."

"Worry? Why, Buddha have mercy! Worries at your age — they cannot be bigger than the head of a poppy seed." Jiiya laughed, and the little wooden clogs rattled in his hands.

"But Jiiya ..." It was no use — for I couldn't even tell him what I had done. "Jiiya, do you know what it's like — to die?"

Jiiya looked surprised. "Die? Really, Little Mistress must not be thinking about such things. What would your honorable mother say if she heard..."

But I didn't pay attention to what he was saying. "I mean, where do you go after you die, Jiiya?" I insisted.

"Where? I will go to *gokuraku* — Buddhist paradise," said Jiiya.

"Is it really a nice place?"

"Of course it is a nice place," said Jiiya, giving a pull at the purple clog thong. "It is full of flowers and five-colored singing birds, and Jiiya will sit on a lotus blossom and look at the silver carp and jade pagodas all day."

After thinking for a while, I made up my mind. "Do you think I can go there too?" I asked.

"Why, Reiko Sama. I thought you were going to that heaven where all those red-haired foreigners go," said Jiiya, a little shortly.

"Jiiya," I said slowly. "I don't think I'll go there."

Jiiya nodded his head gravely, approvingly. "That is good, Little Mistress. Best go where your ancestors are."

"But I don't know whether I can go there either," I said doubtingly.

"Oh yes, you can," said Jiiya. "Our gods aren't that narrow-minded ... When Little Mistress is ready to leave this world, Oshaka Sama — the highest Buddha — will come to greet her on a golden cloud from the western sky. And Jiiya too will come in his train to welcome her."

A little consoled, I made sure of Jiiya's promise. "Would you really come for me? You won't forget, will you, Jiiya?"

"Oh no," said Jiiya, smiling. "Just keep on living with a straightforward spirit, as your ancestors did. There will always be a lotus seat ready and waiting for you in paradise."

Straightforward, I thought, walking back to the house through the tea garden. Hiding things wasn't very straightforward, was it? There were the faded banners and the scarlet armor in the godown. I shouldn't be a coward — for my father's fathers were straightforward and courageous.

That Saturday I went to confession. Father Flaujacque was surprisingly calm when I told him what I had done. He didn't even scold me, but just told me gently not to do it again. And I came out, feeling relieved, and yet curiously empty.

Summer came and went. Autumn deepened, and under the withered chrysanthemums crickets began to sing, "Mend your cloaks, winter is coming." Jiiya was coughing more than usual. He looked tired, and walked slowly and heavily on his bent legs. Finally he was sent away to a hospital, and after that I saw him no more.

When the next *ura bon* — the day of the dead — came, Etsu asked me to accompany her to Jiiya's grave. "Jiiya will be happy if Reiko Sama comes to greet him with a lantern," she said. "He has no relatives here in the city, and the grave is not far..."

All along the street little bonfires were burning at house gates. Monotonous chants of Sutras and the smell of incense wavered up through the dusk into the evening sky. Here and there dark figures with small paper-framed lanterns hurried along to their ancestral graves.

Jiiya was buried in the corner of Kishimojin Cemetery, under a little tombstone. A bunch of faded begonias stood in a bamboo vase, and behind them white wooden tablets with his death name leaned forlornly against the darkening hedge. Etsu threw the flowers away, placed a bowl of cooked rice and vegetables in front of the tombstone, and gave me a kettle with some tea in it.

"I'm sorry, Jiiya," I murmured, pouring tea into the dusty little offering cup. "Now you can't ever come for me with Oshaka Sama on a golden cloud — for I shall have to go to the Foreigners' Heaven after all."

Rain and the Feast
of the Stars

RAIN

THE ROOM is quiet. Only an old-fashioned wall clock ticks away in the shadow. And its round, dull-gold pendulum swings to and fro, to and fro, behind the glass of the black lacquered clock case. On the dais, in front of the picture scroll, an ivory figure of Kwannon, the goddess of mercy, gleams softly, and next to it a pale blue iris bends over the shallow celadon vase. Sunshine, like patches of warm yellow pools, moves from one mat to another, flickering over the painted sliding doors, old cloisonné vases, and my mother's gold-lacquered writing set.

Outside the late afternoon sun yawns, curls up on the lawn, and the weeping cherry tree, clothed in fresh green May leaves, droops over the pond like a tearful nurse. The rhododendrons and azaleas are almost gone; instead the crooked pine trees spread their golden sand on the rocks, and the hedges are buried under the snowy, delicate hare-flowers.

"Would you care for a cup of tea?" I ask. And the slender, willowlike lady in violet kimono nods — faintly. But she doesn't say anything. She keeps on standing stiffly in the tall glass case, holding on to her stained-paper umbrella for dear life, one hand on her narrow black sash. Her high chignon seems to say, very coolly and elegantly, "I really don't care for any, thank you — not that kind of tea, anyway." Oh — well. I turn to the young girl standing on the floor. She is mine — this wisteria maiden, dressed in red twill kimono, with flowing black hair. From under a saffron sedge hat she smiles amiably, winsomely, but her hands are full of purple wisteria flowers. No, she won't do either. There are however others, forming a silent, solemn circle around me. Mary with the golden locks, in pink organdie dress, sits on her cane chair, gazing at the air with huge blue vacant eyes. "Would you like a cup of tea, Mary?" But then I remember the time when I gave her some milk, and since then she stopped saying *"Mamaa"* when I tipped her over.

"Perhaps *you* would like some tea?" I turn to the German doll, Fräulein Roggendorff, named after my honorable piano teacher. She has everything that's real

—real ash-blond hair, pale blue eyes that move and twinkle and close when you put her to bed, arms and legs that bend, so that you can almost make it squat *à la japonaise,* on the matted floor. And her wardrobe—she came with a small trunkful of clothes over the sea, even a velvet-collared coat for Sunday wear. But for all that she is ugly—just a bunch of bones, and horribly real—quite like her namesake, Fräulein Anna Roggendorff.

"It's nothing too special, you know," I say to the doll, imitating my mother's tone. "Just a leaf or two of *Uji* tea—and a piece of very poor bean cake. The powder-pearl tea hasn't arrived on time..." I take hold of Fräulein's neck and help her to some tea from a tiny blue teacup. But she is so clumsy—a drop of green trickles down on her starched white pinafore. *"Aber nein.* Your mannerz are not zo goot, *mein liebes Fräulein."* This time I imitate my piano teacher. "You have not practiced enough—*warum?"* I demand, then add, "Two hours of practice a day—you really should know how to drink tea properly, at your age."

Slowly the sun is leaving the room. Now it's burning a spot on the polished wooden corridor. On the small round tea tray my miniature tea set lies huddled together. Porcelain cups no bigger than my fingertips, a teapot made of passania nut, and a brazier the size of an acorn, wisp of a tea ladle and almost invisible pieces of bean cake that Etsu brought me from the pantry. "This will be all for today," I say, bowing to the silent row of the dolls. "Thank you so much for honoring us with your company — do please come again." After all, there is just so much one can do with dolls...

All this while, Mother has been sitting on her cushion, embroidering. Her face is slightly bent over the lacquered embroidery rack, and her silk sleeve rustles softly as her hand moves up and down, up and down, trailing long threads of gold and silver. I go up behind her to have a look, and there on the black satin a half-finished crane hovers, with a cluster of blue feathers on its head, one silver wing still struggling in the dark... Underneath its feet are the faint white lines of unborn peonies — Mother has the scarlet and green threads out on the rack for them already.

"Mother..."

"What is it, Reiko Chan?" But she does not turn around. And her answer comes from far away, from the edge of the sky where the crane is flying.

"Mother, when is my — governess coming?"

"Your governess?" Mother rests her hand momentarily, and gazes out to the lawn. "Your governess — oh yes, I've almost forgotten." Her hand goes up to her hair, and automatically she adjusts her jade bodkin which is about to fall off. "Next week — most probably." But her voice is still far away.

I am no more enthusiastic about it than Mother. But the idea has hung so long over my head that I am more or less resigned to it — like to the coming long rain in June, or to the frequent colds one suffers in winter. But I must know one thing.

"Mother..."

"What is it, Reiko Chan?" She has gone back to her embroidery. The crane is almost finished — only the tip of its wing is still invisible... Then will come the crimson peonies and the silver clouds.

"Mother, is she going to be — like Fräulein Roggendorff?"

A slow smile appears on her bent profile, and Mother shakes her head. "You silly little child," she says. "Mademoiselle Charlotte is not at all like her — she is a French lady."

A French lady, who is not at all like Fräulein Roggendorff. But the only French lady I knew stood in my sister's room, dressed in a cerise satin gown, with a feathery boa on her arm — her golden hair in a high coiffure, her delicate head a little tilted to the side, a smile on her rosy lips... Would Mademoiselle Charlotte be like that? But how funny — what would Father say if he saw her walking along our dark corridor, beside the paper sliding doors, tugging at her long, heavy, pink satin skirt, a fan in one hand, her head tilted as if ready to burst out singing...

I looked at my Fräulein sitting on the matted floor, limp and lifeless. "Listen," I said sternly. "No more German from now on — you must learn to speak in French, understand? Or else keep absolute silence."

The little doll looked very content to keep quiet.

The evening shadows were slowly descending on the lawn. Only the top of the tall magnolia tree shone in the sunshine, and beside the swing, little white wild orchids began to speckle the dark green brushes. Far away, in the corner of the garden, Father stood under the wisteria arbor, gazing up at the overhanging mass of light purple flowers.

Shall I go out, too? I wondered. But just then Mother looked up, and noticed the solitary figure standing in the soft evening haze. "Again in the garden at this time," she murmured, thrusting the needle into a black pincushion. She stood up, and putting on a pair of sandals went out to the lawn from the corridor.

"Wait for me, Mother..." So seldom I go out to the garden with Mother. But she is gone, walking away toward the arbor.

"Kiyo, Kiyo, my sandals..." How I wish I could hop down to the shoe-off stone, and then to the lawn — the cool, moist grass would feel so nice under my feet...

Kiyo comes scurrying out carrying my little wooden clogs with the scarlet clog thongs. And I run across the lawn after Mother — beneath the *basho* tree, over the mossy steppingstones to the wisteria-covered arbor.

"Your hem, my husband, is soaking wet," my mother was saying. "At this time of the day — you will catch a cold again."

"All right," says Father, but instead of tucking up the hem of his kimono he glances down at the potted dwarf pine. "It needs a little more fertilizer," he murmurs, fingering the tip of a dry, crooked branch. "Looks rather weakened." Then his gaze wanders. "Ah, Reiko," he says, his deep, sunken eyes narrowing into a smile. "Are you studying hard, my child?"

"Yes, Father." There is nothing else to say. Ever

since I can remember, he has always asked me the same question — whether I was reading a picture story-book or playing with the dolls. It's always, "Are you studying hard, my child?"

"Good, good," says Father, nodding. "You will be a great scholar someday."

"Her new governess is coming sometime next week," says Mother.

"Oh." Father sounds vague. "Is she?"

"She is," assures Mother.

"Which one?"

"The French lady whom you engaged through Père Kando," says Mother with an emphasis on "you."

"Hum," says Father, tugging at his mustache. "This dwarf pine..."

"But why must the child be a polyglot?" complains Mother. "None of the other children has ever had foreign tutors."

"That is no reason why *she* shouldn't," says Father.

"It is fine for Reiko to learn flower arrangement or tea ceremony, but French... You know very well she will have to study English when she goes to school. Don't you think it is a little too much of a burden for her age?" Her tone says, "But of course it's no use saying anything now..."

"That is why she should learn to speak other languages at home," replies Father calmly. "Don't worry, the child will forget them all too soon. But it's good to know a little of several things while she is still young."

Mother sighs without a word, but her slender

shoulders seem to say, "I don't know — I don't know whether it is really wise..."

Above us, clusters of lilac-colored blossoms float in the gathering dusk. My mother's kimono half melts into the deep blue shadow, only her face, like a white convolvulus, turns toward the house. "Really, we must be going in," she murmurs. Everything is softer, gentler, blurred — even Father's mustache as he bends down to finger the potted rhodea leaf. The scent of tiny yellow osmanthus clings in the air, heavy, sweet and fragrant. Doves flutter past in the coral-varnished sky, and outside our high stone wall echoes the song of children going home — their voices rise high and clear, singing the song of evening and setting sun, and the burning, cinnabarred clouds...

June came, and with it the long, endless rain. Day after day dawned on the silver-gray sky, and with the quiet whisper of raindrops upon the roof. Beside the pond stood the willows, wreathed in pearl-colored fume, and on the wrinkled water, under the silky threads of rain, the white lotus flowers swayed gently. Pebbles shone wet on the graveled path leading to our gate, and green baby frogs leaped in the new-made stream.

Day after day I spent at home, playing with Etsu, reading, practicing the piano, while the rain splashed on the lawn outside, and a silvery light gleamed on the swing and the treetops. "I wish," said Mother, "your governess would arrive if she is going to come at all."

Then one misty afternoon Mademoiselle Charlotte's luggage arrived. One large trunk, several suitcases of black leather, with labels in different languages, sizes and colors stamped all over them. "The lady must have traveled a great deal," said Etsu, wiping waterdrops off the shining metals. "It must be so exciting..." The luggage brought in a curious smell — smell of wet leather, wax and salty breeze. They sat in our hall like a group of silent strangers, then Saku, our gardener, carried them upstairs — to the guest room which was to be hers. But still no trace of Mademoiselle Charlotte.

Fräulein Roggendorff wasn't at all like that. She was the soul of punctuality. Even if the rain washed away all the roads in Tokyo — and every Wednesday night I prayed that it would — she would still have stood in front of our high wooden stoop, ringing the bell as if it were a clarion call. Even when the rain was pouring, and little brooks ran on both sides of the road, and children went singing, splashing in their rubber boots, she would be seen in front of our high, tile-ridged gate, walking up and down, up and down, with her big, rapid stride — because she had gotten there too early, and she didn't want to come in before the appointed hour. Clad in a white gabardine raincoat, a pair of black galoshes, a dripping umbrella in her hand, she looked like a rain-soaked Brünhilde.

And at exactly five minutes after two I would be seated in front of the Bechstein, running my unsteady fingers over the ivory keyboard, while she would stand beside me, her hands clasped behind, beating time with her deep, hollow voice. *"Ein, zwei, drei, ein, zwei, drei — aber nein, mein Gott!* You do not play like that — not Bach!" Then her eyes, under the shaggy gray brows, would gleam bottomless. *"G-dur, G-dur, hast du vergessen?"*

She sits down on the stool and begins playing. The little piece becomes alive, running up and down the keyboard like a graceful mouse, then turning deep, broad, melancholy — almost tender...

"Once more please." Bach's Inventions — such tiny little pieces, but oh, so difficult. Why can't I play something like the Flower Song, or Beethoven's Minuet? The clock ticks on the mantelpiece, and outside the unceasing patter of rain against the windowpane. The bamboo leaves waver against the wall, wet and gleaming, and a little green caterpillar crawls on the window sill. Behind me strides Fräulein Roggendorff, her hands on her back, keeping time. How large her feet are, clad in coarse brown leather boots.

Clementi's Sonatine is much easier — it escapes through my fingers like a strand of pearls, a little unevenly, but lightly and quickly.

"Ein, zwei, drei, vier — keep the correct time," says the voice from behind. "Don't let it run away..."

Oh let it run away, and the time too... When can I get over with all this? When am I going to be able to play as my brother does — so easily, so happily? Or why can't I learn to play the silken-stringed lyre as my sister does — her teacher is so gentle, polite, and always smiling... The green baby frogs must be singing in the pond, and the willows nodding in the rain, and the wet silverberries shining against the fresh green leaves...

"*Ein, zwei, drei,*" the clock tinkles on the mantelpiece. And the Fräulein pulls out a large, round watch from her pocket as if to make sure. "All right," she says reluctantly. "That is all for today." Then she smiles, for the first time. "You did not play too badly, mein liebes Fräulein — you have made *some* progress. Do keep it up."

I make a hasty bow and retreat through the heavy oak sliding door. Now Mother will have tea with the Fräulein and talk about the Church — let the grownups tend to it. Let them talk and entertain each other... I go back to my room, but Etsu isn't there.

"Etsu — where's Etsu?"

"She is in the godown, Reiko Sama," says Kiyo, wiping her hands with an apron. "She is looking for something to put into your governess's room."

Down the corridor, out through the glass door, across the garden under the rain to the godown. Its big wrought-iron door is half open, and a moldy smell greets me as I go in.

"Etsu, where are you?"

"Here, Reiko Sama," a silvery voice comes floating through the dark. "Be careful — there are things on the floor."

In the corner stands Etsu, bending over an old paulownia cabinet, a white cloth on her hair. She turns around and smiles. "What do you think, Reiko Sama," she inquires, wiping the top of the cabinet with an oily cloth. "Do you think this will do for — the foreign guest?"

I look at it solemnly and nod. But I am not sure. The cabinet is very, very Japanese — how is Mademoiselle Charlotte going to put her pink satin skirt with a hoop in it? Her boas, her fans and her hat with long ostrich feather?

"Don't we have a wardrobe like the one in my sister's room?" I ask hesitantly. "You know, something a little larger — so that she could hang her dresses up?"

"The clothespress is in her room already," replies Etsu. "This is just for small things."

Small things — yes, of course. I think of my mother's jewelry box, lace handkerchiefs and green jadeite sash bands. But Mademoiselle Charlotte would have something else — lace handkerchiefs, yes, but no sash bands. Perhaps dozens and dozens of gloves, perfume and smelling-salt bottles. "She can put her fans in this," I decide. And Etsu agrees, trying not to smile.

But soon my attention wanders away from the little white cabinet, for there are so many other things to see. "Etsu, open this box, will you?"

The box is large and square, with engraved corners and a big iron latch. The lid opens with a heavy groan, and underneath the turmeric-colored cloth lies a set of embroidered clothes.

"Your great-grandmother's bridal costume," says Etsu, who knows all about my family history. But they are so big and heavy looking — covered thick with gold, silver, and dark-crimson lacquered threads. The whole kimono is one big picture scroll, which reminds me of our old manservant Jiiya's paradise — round, red bridges, crystal rivers and coral pagodas, five-colored birds called Kalavinka. Sashes of figured brocade lie like glittering rivers coiled up in the shadowy chest, and around them are scattered a cinnamon-colored tobacco tray, ornamental bodkins and tortoise-shell combs, small bead-tree boxes and silver hairpins with embossed carving. And behind the chest stands a crimson clothesrack, much taller than the one in my mother's room.

In oblong white-wood boxes are kept the swords. One by one Etsu opens the lids and lifts the long, gently curving swords, then draws them carefully out of their scabbards. The blades shine cold and blue in the darkness, like shafts of moonbeam on pure, deep water. But there is a brown stain on one of them.

"What is this, Etsu — why is this rusty?"

But Etsu doesn't answer. Quietly, she puts it away, back into the sheath and then to the box.

From one of the smaller chests decorated with our paulownia crest comes a faded, moth-eaten scroll.

"Your family tree," says Etsu, unfolding the paper. "Yasumasa, the first Lord of Oyama Castle..." Slowly, clearly, Etsu reads the names out loud. But those are just names — names of people who lived three, four hundred years ago.

Rolling back the scroll, Etsu says softly, "But this is just a copy."

"Where is the real one then?" I ask.

"In Ibaragi, at your uncle's home."

"Why?"

"Because the original must remain in the country of your family seat."

"Why aren't we there, Etsu? Why don't we ever go there?"

"Because your honorable father preferred the new Western world," says Etsu. And somehow, the new Western world looms in my mind in the figures of Fräulein Roggendorff and Mademoiselle Charlotte — in her pink satin gown and her feathery boa . . . Oh yes, the cabinet.

"I will ask Saku to bring up this one then," says Etsu.

"Have some more coffee?" asks Father very politely.

"Mais oui, merci mille fois," says Mademoiselle Charlotte, handing her cup over to Toki, who stands behind her chair with a coffeepot.

Poor Mademoiselle, I think, sipping my bean soup. Breakfast must be the only meal she enjoys, for we have a choice — a choice between toast, eggs, ham and coffee, or bean soup, blue laver, pickles and rice. But lunch and dinner are quite often Japanese. Does she like Japanese food? I wonder, then decide she doesn't. That must be why she is so thin . . .

"Marmalade?" asks Mother, a little nervously.

"Ah, merci," replies Mademoiselle Charlotte brightly, smiling. "But this is excellent — this marmalade."

"We made it at home," informs Mother, relieved.

"Oh, yes? My mother — God bless her — used to make it too, *chez nous, à Montpellier,*" says Mademoiselle

Charlotte, then turns to Father. "Monsieur, have you been to Montpellier? Southern France? Marseille?"

"Much as I regret..." begins my father, but he is interrupted. "Ah yes, I have forgotten — you have been to America, but not in Europe, *n'est ce pas?*"

"No — but I intend to send her there eventually — to England perhaps," says Father, giving me a nod.

"That will be charming," says Mademoiselle Charlotte. "But why not to France?"

"Oh, one of the boys might go," says Father casually. "If he wants to."

"But of course," says Mademoiselle Charlotte, spreading butter delicately on a piece of toast. "One should visit there sometime..."

My brothers and sisters have left for school a long time ago, and the dining room is very quiet. The rain has stopped for a short while, and the faint sunshine flickers on the lace window curtains, and traces a pattern on the wooden mosaic floor. Outside, the ground is softly steaming, and dewdrops glisten on the broad cycad leaves. The sky is veiled with thin, opaline clouds, and the air is warm, damp, breathless. Mademoiselle Charlotte sits facing the garden, peeling an amber-colored loquat. She is small, slender, with soft brown hair and greenish eyes, and a nose which is a trifle too long. Bending over the mahogany table, in a gray crepe de Chine blouse, she looks like a little squirrel with an acorn.

"How long have you been in the Orient?" asks Mother.

"Almost ten years," replies my teacher. "I was on my way to Tahiti — then I stopped here, and stayed."

"Will you be going home someday?" asks Mother again.

Mademoiselle Charlotte shrugs her shoulders very faintly. "I don't know..." Her gaze wanders over to the garden. A dewdrop falls and splashes on the window sill. Shadow of a cloud flits over the lawn, and a piece of juicy, golden loquat lies in the blue and white porcelain dish in front of Mademoiselle, a little forlornly. *"Qui sait?"* she repeats softly...

But how the upstairs room has changed! There is a deep-blue carpet on the floor, damask curtains and a faded Gobelin tapestry, embroidered cushions on the armchair, and an etching of Reims Cathedral on the wall. A bed with carved posts, and next to it is the paulownia cabinet, with a statue of Our Lady, a missal, and a picture of a young man in a white linen suit.

"My fiancé," says Mademoiselle Charlotte. *"C'est-à-dire,* he was."

"Oh..."

"But he is dead," she continues gently. *"A Tahiti."* She looks down through the open window, to the wide green lawn, to the pond and the stream, and the mounds covered with camellia trees, then to the veiled indigo sky beyond. The gentleman in white, with light-colored mustache, looks out of the frame indifferently. "It was a long time ago," says Mademoiselle Charlotte. But she doesn't look sad at all. She turns around and smiles. "And now, we shall go back to our lesson," she says.

We have just gotten through "July the Fourteenth" with its *drapeau tri-colore,* processions, and the fireworks on the Seine. Next comes *"La Vacance de Jeanne."* Mademoiselle Charlotte speaks rapidly — very rapidly, like an incessant, rippling stream that runs down over the moss-covered rocks. And most of the time I don't understand what she is saying. Only when she reads, her voice becomes soft and dreamy, full of sighs...

"Au bord de la mer," she reads slowly, *"le ciel était tout bleu, la terre était toute verte. Jeanne, avec son chien Fido..."* I fidget on my small hard-backed chair. I think of my dog, Daru. He must be sitting on the kitchen floor, his bushy tail curled up, following Kiyo's movements with his black, pensive eyes. But he doesn't run around like Fido — he is very large and languid, with coarse white hair and... Mademoiselle looks up. *"Vous êtes fatiguée, Thérèse?"* she asks. Thérèse — she calls me by my christian name. *Thérèse, ma petite fleur, ma fille...* I have gotten used to these endearing terms already. But sometimes she calls me Mademoiselle Champignon, because she thinks my head looks like a mushroom — but that is of course when my mother is not within hearing.

"Assez," says Mademoiselle Charlotte, closing her book. Good thing, she never insists... "Don't forget the seven exceptions to the *'ou'*-ending nouns. Now, come around here for a minute."

Obediently I go around the desk and stand next to her chair. There is a big map opened on the desk, and putting her arm around my shoulders, my governess whispers, *"Voilà Montpellier."* But all I can see is a dot on the edge of a sprawling blue sea. *"Au bord de la Meditérranée,"* she murmurs. *"Ah, que c'est beau, mon pays..."* My black, straight hair brushes against her shoulders, and a long, white, bony finger trembles on the edge of the map. For a long time she gazes at the tiny dot without a word, and her profile with the long nose looks far away and dreamy.

The ivy leaves sigh gently outside the french window, and the crape myrtle rustles in the breeze. From the groves floats up the scent of *passania* flowers. Shadows fall on the desk, and the air becomes cool and heavy under the gathering clouds. The rains are returning.

Abruptly my teacher looks up. "You may go now — run along, *ma chère Thérèse,*" she says, and gives me a kiss. This is something new that I have to get used to — and going out of the room, I resist the temptation to put a finger up to my cheek, which still feels moist and a little sticky...

THE FEAST OF THE STARS

Little by little the rains became lighter. Deep azure sky began to peep from between the clouds, and in our garden young leaves burned bright green under the sparkling sun. The pomegranate tree spread its scarlet sundew over the moist, black ground, and the white gardenias began to bloom near the sedge. At the back of Father's study, short, hairy bamboo shoots grew up into slender, pale green saplings, and over them tall, feathery mother-bamboos swayed and rustled in the early summer breeze.

"Which one shall we choose?" asks Mother, standing near the wicket in her light blue crepe kimono, a pair of scissors in her hand. Which one? But there are so many from which to choose — some barely reaching my shoulder, one ten times taller than I am, with broad shining leaves bordered with white, trembling under the morning dew. Gently I reach out with my finger to touch the strong, round, knuckled stem, faintly covered with ivory-colored powder — it feels so smooth and cool...

"Perhaps this will do," says Mother, tapping lightly with her scissors one of the medium-sized bamboos. "I must tell Saku to plant this one in a pot."

Just then the round paper-screened window behind us slid open and Father's mustached face appeared. "Oh, it's you," he says. "I wondered who — what is the matter?"

"We are choosing a bamboo for the Feast of the Stars tonight," says Mother. Have you forgotten? This is the seventh of July."

"Oh yes." Father sounds noncommittal.

Tonight we are going to have the celebration of the stars — for this is the only night in the year when the Herdsman crosses the Celestial River to meet the fair Weaving Maid. Saku will plant the bamboo in a large earthenware pot, and we will decorate it with different-colored papers, straw balls and little tinkling bells, then sit in the garden and write poems to honor the two unfortunate stars...

"What do you think of this one?" asks Mother, touching the medium-sized bamboo she chose.

"Fine, fine," says Father, very agreeably but without paying much attention. After glancing over the dew-covered garden and his dwarf plants, Father settles down to his reading again.

"Father, when are we going to the sea?" I ask, pulling at a bamboo leaf. The school is over for my brothers and sisters, and it has been decided this year for us to go to the sea. But, "I am not going," says Father. "It will be too noisy there..." Then turning to Mother, "You can take the children, and leave Kiyo."

Mother keeps silence. After all, Kamakura isn't too far — she can come back to Tokyo almost every day for that matter...

"Is Mademoiselle Charlotte coming with us too?" I ask.

"Of course," says Mother, matter-of-factly. "You might as well continue your lessons once you've started."

At this Father looks up from his book. "How are your studies, Reiko? Have you made much progress?" he asks.

"I don't know, Father. Mademoiselle Charlotte speaks so quickly..."

"You will get used to it," says Father. "Don't worry — when I first went to America..."

"But really, what is she going to do?" interrupts Mother, turning around from the bamboo bush. "She can't live abroad all her life — don't you think Reiko should have an education given to any other Japanese girl her age?"

"There is plenty of time for that too," replies Father calmly. "Besides, why should she follow a set pattern of life just because everyone else does — unless it makes her happier?" There is a tone of irony in his voice.

"No, but it might mean less unhappiness," replies Mother, a little meaningfully.

Traditional ways and foreign culture, different sets of values — all those words mean very little to me. It is more important to think of the poem I have to compose this evening. Stars — two bright white stars facing each other across the River of Heaven, the Weaving Maiden dressed in light silk tunic and a flowing skirt, and the Herdsman with pointed-toe sandals, leading a milk-white cow ... The picture is very pretty, but I don't know how to make it into a poem.

The bamboo bush rustles, and Etsu comes around from the back yard.

"Reiko Sama's piano teacher has arrived," she says with a smile.

"Oh yes, the piano ..." Mother sounds faintly surprised. "I didn't realize it was so late."

"Don't let the teacher wait," says Father. "It would be impolite."

"Etsu, show Miss Roggendorff into the parlor, and change Reiko's kimono. I'll be there in a minute."

Mother walks away, under the slanting eaves, over the steppingstones, back to her room still with a pair of scissors in her hand.

Slowly I go along the hedge, reluctant to go inside. Sunshine pours over my back, warm and clinging. Beside the swing huge yellow sunflowers lift their heads languidly toward the sky. And above, a little white cloud sails away in the blue. Someday, I think, I too will sail away across the sea, to visit all the strange places on Mademoiselle Charlotte's map—across the different-colored seas to visit those tiny little dots... Light footsteps are heard inside the house, and Etsu's white apron appears in the corridor.

"Please come in, Reiko Sama," she says, shielding her eyes with one hand against the glare of the sun. "Your piano teacher is waiting."

"All right," says Fräulein Roggendorff, but she does not add, "This is all for today." For today is the last day she will be here. Instead, she takes off her horn-rimmed glasses and wipes them with her big white handkerchief. "You will not be playing the piano during summer, will you?" she inquires a little sadly.

"I don't think so, Fräulein Roggendorff."

"Too bad," my teacher shakes her head. "Too bad— piano is something one has to keep at continuously —otherwise one loses one's technique."

I don't know what "technique" means, but nod seriously to be polite. The alabaster clock squats silently on the mantelpiece — Toki has forgotten to wind it again. The weather is getting quite warm and through the open window a breeze comes in and ruffles the pages of my music book. On the white lace tablecloth stands a deep-blue vase, tall and slender, shining in spots like a zircon, holding a crimson, long-stemmed rose. Out on the lawn, trees with their leaves already turning dark green droop in the burning sun. Isn't she going to let me go? I wonder, standing beside the piano stool.

But instead of dismissing me as usual, Fräulein Roggendorff goes to the window and looks outside. "You have a beautiful garden," she says quietly. "Beautiful trees..." Her short, gray-brown hair falls on her forehead, and she brushes it away, a little irritably. In her coarse woolen jacket, flannel skirt and cotton stockings, she looks like an aged oak tree.

Suddenly she strides back to the table and picks up the crimson rose. *"Du bist wie eine Blume,"* she recites softly with a half-smile. But this is so sudden that the little flower trembles in her large, bony hand. "This rose doesn't have enough fragrance," says the Fräulein, putting it back in the vase. "Our roses — in Rhineland..." Then she turns to me and says severely, "Girls in Rhineland have braids...blond or chestnut-colored braids." And she stares at my short black hair intently through her thick glasses. I am beginning to feel a bit uneasy. This is so strange — the first time she has spoken of anything except our piano lessons...

The door slides open and in comes Mother followed by Toki. Rum babas and Ceylon tea — the white and gold teacups tinkle quietly on the tray, and the long-necked silver teapot glistens in the sunshine.

"Reiko will have tea with us today, for this is the last time," says Mother, sitting down.

Cups are filled, passed around, and Mother begins talking with Fräulein Roggendorff. "I might send her to school next year," says Mother. I look up quickly. This is a surprise. "It isn't true, is it, Mother?" I want to say, but keep quiet.

"Ah, zo," says the Fräulein without expression. "It might be a good idea — her brothers are in the Gymnasium, are they not, Mrs. Hatsumi?"

Good idea — why ... I feel quite indignant toward my piano teacher. Of all the things to say ...

"She is already past the age for the first year of primary school," explains Mother. "But her father objected to sending her — Sacred Heart is so far. Unless we put her into the boarding house ..."

Boarding house — suddenly the rum baba loses its taste in my mouth, and the green tea becomes lukewarm and bitter. But Mother continues unconcernedly. "If not, then perhaps she will resume her lessons after summer." But somehow, we all feel that it is not to be — why, no one knows.

"Of course, if you wish," says the Fräulein, bending over the teacup. But something about her stooped shoulders says *"Ich bin verlassen — Ich bin verlassen."*

"You may go now, Reiko Chan," says Mother. I stand up and bow, while my teacher turns around and stretches out her arm. Dear me — is she going to kiss me too? For a moment I feel panic-stricken. But no — instead she shakes hands with me, as if I were a grown *Frau*, and not a little girl at all. Her grasp feels strangely warm and friendly. But, *"Auf wiedersehen,* have a nice holiday," says her voice as though arising from a grave. "Don't forget to keep time when you play," she adds, dropping my hand.

"Continue with the leaves," says Mademoiselle Charlotte. "After you are finished with all of them I will show you how to make the flowers."

I don't mind embroidery — it is a slow, painstaking thing to do, but I can let my mind wander while I work.

"I will read to you — yes?" says Mademoiselle Charlotte, settling back in her chair and taking up her book.

From time to time the breeze rustles in the sultan's parasol outside the window. The shadow of the leaves falls on the curtains, tracing an arabesque of pale and dark green. Everything is very soft in this room — the light that flickers in from the window, the gray and blue curtains and the bedspread, and the faded Gobelin tapestry. In a quiet voice Mademoiselle Charlotte reads on.

Ainsi, toujours poussés vers de nouveaux rivages,
Dans la nuit eternelle emportés sans retour,
Ne pourrons-nous jamais sur l'océan des ages
  Jeter l'ancre un seul jour?

"Ah," she sighs, falling back for a moment on her chair, and her silk blouse flutters like a sail in the breeze.

"Mademoiselle," I interrupt. "May I ask you a question?"

"*Mais certainement,*" she says, coming back to this world. "*Qu'est ce que c'est, ma fille?*"

"Do all the girls — in France — wear their hair in braids?" I ask.

"That depends — not always. But why?" Mademoiselle replies, looking interested.

"Fräulein Roggendorff said that girls in Rheinland do . . ."

"*Mon Dieu* — perhaps in Rheinland. In Germany — one can expect anything," says Mademoiselle Charlotte. "But in France, girls have long curly hair, especially on Sundays, when they go to church."

I go back to my work, and she begins reading again, this time a little more loudly.

But before long she is interrupted again. There is a noise in the garden below. Saku has just dug up the medium-sized bamboo and brought it around in a pot to the front lawn. "What is that?" inquires my teacher, looking out from the window down to the blue cotton livery of Saku hovering around the potted bamboo.

"*Tanabata* — Seventh Eve," I tell her. But she still looks puzzled. So I begin to explain the story, in halting French, of how the two unfortunate stars offended the Emperor of Heaven, and were decreed to live apart forever, except to meet once a year on the seventh night of the seventh moon. Mademoiselle Charlotte listens attentively, smiling. Moreover, she helps me from time to time, as if she knew all about the story already.

"And so, they are going to cross the Celestial River this evening, and we have to decorate the bamboo tree and write poems about them," I conclude, and feel hot and shy all of a sudden. So far, I have never spoken more than a sentence at a time to my teacher. And now — wasn't it unbecoming for a little girl to talk so much to her teacher?

"You have told it beautifully," says Mademoiselle Charlotte, still smiling. Then she adds, "It is a beautiful story too." For some reason or other she looks happy. And after a pause she says, "I too came across the water, only it wasn't the Celestial River, but an ocean. And instead of meeting the Herdsman, I met my little Thérèse." I look down, feeling confused. I don't know what to say... Could I say I am happy too that she came across the ocean? But it might not be respectful enough... So in silence I go back to my embroidery, and Mademoiselle Charlotte takes up her book again.

Tick, tock, says the clock. The dull-gold pendulum swings to and fro. On the dais stands a tall, ivory-colored flower with a faint crimson lining. The silk sitting cushions are changed to hemp-leaf ones, and from the wooden frieze strip hangs a wind bell. In front of the lacquered writing desk sits Mother, with a bamboo-stemmed brush in her hand. On her desk are scattered clusters of different-colored papers, which I have carefully cut into an oblong shape. While I sit in the corridor, making more and more of them, Mother's voice, low and melodious, pauses over a half-formed verse, repeating the same word over and over again.

Next to me squats Fräulein Roggendorff, this time in her Sunday wear. I have decided to take her to the seaside with me — for some unknown reason, the doll has become my favorite since this morning. And I wonder, if I am going to a boarding school, whether I could take her along with me...

"Mother." I call her softly, so as not to disturb her too much. "Mother, am I going to school next year?"

She turns around. "I don't know," she says vaguely. "We'll have to think about it a while yet..." Then she picks up the poem I wrote, and reads it in silence. As she puts the paper down on the desk, a frown appears on her forehead. "Really — your calligraphy," she sighs. "Have you done your brush writing today?"

"No, Mother."

"What are you going to be when you grow up?" Mother wonders. "With this handwriting..."

Offhand, I don't want to be anything. I just want to stay as I am. Only if Mother would play with me a little more...

A telephone bell rings somewhere far, then stops abruptly, as if someone has put a lid on it in a hurry. I have finished cutting enough colored papers to deco-rate five bamboo trees, and wonder when we are going to begin the celebration. Right after supper, perhaps — it's so nice to have everyone together, talking and laughing. And it so seldom happens...Perhaps when we are at the seaside Mother would have more time. I look at my Fräulein sitting beside me in the corridor.

She needs a bathing suit — and a parasol too, since I broke her old one.

"Mother, my doll needs a parasol for the beach..." But the paper partition slides open and Kiyo kneels on the threshold. "Telephone, Mistress," she says.

Mother is gone, and I make a face at the Fräulein. "*Patience, ma fille,*" I say, trying to sound like Mademoiselle Charlotte. "You would like a parasol — no? You would look very elegant..." But somehow the soft sound of French does not agree with the stiffly tailored coat of Fräulein Roggendorff. And I go back to my half-forgotten German. "*Die Rheinischen Mädchen,*" I repeat, "all have braids." Then I peer through my imaginary glasses and say, "Now, why don't *you* have braids?" The Fräulein's hair is short and stringy, but perhaps I could make it into braids if I had a piece of ribbon.

The clock ticks on. And the afternoon is growing old. The drowsy warmth and the sunshine are slowly floating away. Leaves twinkle in the slanting sun, and huge masses of clouds pass leisurely over the pine-covered mounds.

Mother comes back, but the Fräulein and the parasol are both forgotten. "Kiyo, Kiyo," she calls, clapping her hands. "I have to go out — there's a tea gathering at Mrs. Hara's home..."

Quickly, deftly, Kiyo arranges Mother's kimono. And after a while Mother stands in the middle of her dressing room, ready to go out. Russet silk, with silver flowers on the hem, and an agate sash band in the shape of a carp — Mother stands, smoothing her hair before the mirror.

"Mother, when will you be home?"

"I don't know — not too late, I hope."

"Would you bring me back — something nice?"

"Yes, Reiko Chan." Then she goes away, leaving everything on the floor. Toki will have to fold them away, carefully, into the paulownia wardrobe. The sound of the car grows farther and farther away... "*Patience, ma fille,*" I say to the Fräulein again. But I know better. Mother always forgets to bring me home "something nice." Best not to expect anything — then I won't be so disappointed...

For a long, long time I sat in the corridor, hugging my knees with both hands, all alone. Slowly, gradually, the sun went down, casting its golden rays over the still, dark trees. The zaffer blue sky turned pink, became colorless, then was dyed into a deep indigo shade. Bats began to skim through the shadowy groves, and from the faraway woods of the Myojin Shrine the sad voice of an owl came echoing in the falling dusk. Above, the little stars began to sparkle in the mazarine sky, and in front of Mother's room the bamboo tree stood, with all its colored papers, bells and straw balls faintly shining in their light.

"Thérèse — Mademoiselle Champignon," a voice calls from the far end of the corridor. "Thérèse — *venez vite.* I have something nice for you . . ." The voice trails off into the deepening shadow in the corridor.

133. Rain and the Feast of the Stars

I pick up my doll and go out of the room. Outside, our garden stretches, with waves of moving trees and murmuring grass, fading far into the deep, dark ocean of the night. Going up the stairs, I decide to introduce the Fräulein to my French governess. And, straightening her collar, I say softly to the doll, "You might have a new *maman* — perhaps, if she likes..."

Going
to School

THE GARDEN looked the same. But as I walked up the little path beneath the camellia trees to the pond, I noticed an almost invisible change. Autumn had come. The twisted rose vine clung forlornly to the hedge, and the curly brown fuchsia leaves lay scattered on the ground. Only the pine trees, as bent and gaunt as ever, stretched their crooked boughs over the stream. The lawn had changed from the burning green of two months ago to a softer hue, looking pale and yellow under the late afternoon sun; and I remembered, a little sadly, how soft and springy it felt then under my shoes. But now the grass was hard and dry, like a worn-out carpet about to crumble away.

The pond lay deserted, half hidden in the shade. The wind and the rain had swept the fallen leaves to one side, and on the still emerald-green surface tiny water spiders traced a vanishing pattern. From across the pond, on the shaggy, moss-covered rocks, the red, round, juicy berries beckoned — "Here we are, come around and taste us..." But they are bitter and, so I have been told, poisonous. "How do you do," said the white bush clover from under the bending willow tree. "My, how you have grown — but no wonder, it's been such a long time since we saw you last."

I turn away, feeling, I don't know exactly why, sad and listless. Or is it because I have just come back, and will have to go away so very soon?

Go away — Mother would have said if she heard me, with, as usual, her slightly raised eyebrows. But why? What a funny child you are. You sound as if you are leaving us forever, and not coming back. After all, you are just going to be a day scholar. You'll be home every day.

But still it's not the same, I think, fingering the rough bark of a pine tree and watching the amber-colored sap trickling down from between the black scales like a heavy, golden teardrop. Leave home every day? Leave all my dolls, my books, and go away into a strange world? Suddenly a cold wind blows past me, and I shiver. School, a place unknown, far away, full of strange children, strange things... Being the youngest of the family, I am used to grownups, but I am afraid of children my own age.

Perhaps I could ask Father not to send me away, I tell myself, kneeling down beside the mossy edge of the pond. Perhaps he will understand — if I promised to study very hard at home. But what if he said no... Through the trees the little stream flows away. Shadow of a cloud falls on the still water, and the thin willow tree sheds its leaves one by one noiselessly in the wind.

But what if he said no... The pond looks cold, deep, and secretive. And I remember the story of how once my brother was almost drowned in its water. What is it like to die? It must be like going to a deep deep sleep and never waking up — a very deep sleep, not even with dreams...

Hesitantly, I put a finger into the water, to see how cold it might be. Then a huge golden carp comes swishing up from the green depths, turns a somersault and disappears again. The little white cloud is torn to a thousand shreds, and I look up, startled. "Reiko Sama..." Somewhere, someone is calling. It must be teatime. Suddenly I feel hungry, and standing up, I begin walking toward the house, first slowly, then skipping and running across the lawn.

A light from the paper-framed lamp beside Father's writing desk fell trembling on the lacquered fancy shelf. In the corner, on the dais, studded sword hilts glistened somberly against the wall. Outside, the crape myrtle stood, its huge leaves folded against each other in the shadow. And far away, the faint murmur of the stream sounded, like tiny footsteps running away into the dark.

"Father," I called hesitantly. He didn't stir.

"Father," I called again, a little more loudly.

Slowly he looked up and turned his head, peering into the shadow where I stood. "Ah, Reiko," he said, faintly surprised. "What is the matter — do you want something?"

"Father," I said, crouching down on the edge of the matted floor, "why must I go to school?"

"School?" His eyes wandered past me to the dimly lit alcove. "What school?"

"Sacred Heart, Father."

"Oh yes," he murmured, putting down his pen. "Is it time for that already?"

"Mother said I have to go tomorrow..."

"Is that so? Well, well," said Father, pulling at his mustache. He sounded amiable, but like a stranger.

"Father," I began again. A tremble crept into my voice, and I couldn't keep it still. "Must I really go to school?"

Father looked at me, this time more interestedly. "Why, Reiko? Don't you want to go?"

"No, Father."

"Why not?" he asked, still looking at me, very gently.

"I — don't know," I faltered. Father relapsed into silence, while his eyes traveled back to the books on his desk. The little lamp threw a circle of light on the polished sandalwood, shining like a patch of dark violet water. My father kept such a long silence that I began to wonder whether he had forgotten me.

"I'll study very hard if you will let me stay at home, Father," I insisted without much hope.

"All right," he said finally. "If you don't want to go."

"Really, Father?" My heart gave a big jump. Oh, what a relief it was...

"Good night, Reiko, study hard," said Father, without turning around. His voice sounded remote, and a bit tired.

But the next morning Etsu woke me up quite early. And when I opened my eyes the first thing I saw was my school uniform, neatly laid out on the bedside chair.

"Why, Etsu, I am not going to school, you know." I closed my eyes and turned over to the other side of the bed, feeling lazy and comfortable.

"But Reiko Sama — the Mistress told me to come and dress you now..."

"Go and ask Father, Etsu, and stop bothering me." It was so lovely to go back to sleep, to let myself sink into the soft, enveloping shadow. It was just like floating on the sea, lulled and caressed by the rolling, gentle waves...

"But Reiko Sama..."

"Oh, go away, Etsu. And draw the curtain again, will you?" The sea at Kamakura must be waking up now, yawning under the first ray of the sun, and the fishermen drawing up their morning catch... The clouds will be burning on the pale blue horizon, and the sunshine sparkling on the water like powder of gold...The breeze will be cold, and smelling of salt and the seaweed. The big, wooden, angular fishermen's boats will be silhouetted dark against the shimmering orange dawn light, and the lithe, brown village children skipping and shouting, racing among the nets. And on the seashore, after each wave comes and goes, the pink, delicate cherry-shells half buried in the wet clinging sand...

The door opens and Mother comes in.

"Why, good morning, Mother." There is something wrong, I feel, slowly and reluctantly waking up again. Mother *never* comes into my room at this hour. As a matter of fact, she seldom comes into my room, if ever.

Mother stands at the foot of my bed and looks at me. She is fully dressed, and there are two faint lines on her white forehead. "It's getting late, Reiko Chan," she says, then turns to the window. "Look, the sun is high up already. Why, you used to get up so early at Kamakura."

"Yes, Mother." But she doesn't know the difference. At Kamakura, long before this time of the day, my cousin will be calling under the window with his fishing rod. And we'll be walking, hand in hand, on the long, white, deserted path covered with sand, among the pine trees, down to the sea...

"Reiko," Mother repeats. And this time there is a light tone of irritation in her voice. "You had better get up now. Remember, this is your first day at school."

I wake up with an uncomfortable suddenness. "But Mother, I'm not going to school. Father said I didn't have to."

Mother turns away for a moment, but her hand on the thin, dark-brown bedpost tightens its grip. Her eyes travel to the window, to the maple leaves shining in the sun. "Anyway," she says a bit airily, "you had better get up now. After all, you aren't a baby anymore, you realize..."

The car went through the white marble gate, and along an avenue of cherry trees. On both sides stretched a tangle of brushes, and above the hill, among the trees, the pointed chapel tower shone bronze-colored in the autumn sky. How funny, I thought, pressing my face on the windowpane. Only a few minutes ago we were in the city — and now, this is just like our country house...

We were on our way to school, "for a visit," as Mother put it. For she had promised Reverend Mother that we'd be there today, and promises were, of course, very serious things.

After a while our car swung around the curve, sped up the slope to a graveled court flanked by a tall shingled building, and stopped in front of its ivy-covered porte-cochere. The chauffeur sprang down, opened the door and bowed. "Wait for me, Kikuchi," said Mother casually. "We shan't be long..."

The drawing room was quite dark, and the air chilly. A stray bit of sunshine that came in from the hall lay on the table like a speck of yellow dust. In the corner, on a shelf, statues of saints stood, dim and immobile, silently praying. At the opposite end of the table sat

Reverend Mother, quiet and dignified, with dark gray, austere eyes. Only when she smiled, quite unexpectedly, her face became soft—almost shy. Next to her sat another nun, thin and gentle looking.

How long are we going to stay here? I wondered, sitting on the edge of a hard leather chair, getting bored. Aren't we ever going to leave? But they continued talking, rapidly, seriously, occasionally glancing at me and nodding.

"Come here, dear." Suddenly Reverend Mother turned and stretched a hand toward me. Obediently I walked over and stood beside her chair. "The child's uniform is too short, Mrs. Hatsumi," said Reverend Mother, and bending down, she indicated with her hand how my navy blue skirt should be lengthened.

"Yes, of course. I will have it altered right away."

I wondered what for. Were we going to come here for a visit again? Somewhere a bell rang, and from the far end of the building, millions of little footsteps came echoing. And soon a procession of shadows fell across the glass door—shadows of veiled figures like a string of fleeing ghosts...Small, hurried footsteps continued to sound in the corridor and then grew fainter.

"It's the hour of devotion," said Reverend Mother, standing up. "I will take her to the chapel myself, Mrs. Hatsumi."

"Thank you, Reverend Mother." My mother stood up also, folding her fan. "You'll be a good child, Reiko, and not give any trouble to the good Mothers..."

But this is so sudden, so unexpected..."Are you going, Mother?" Please don't leave me here, with these strange people...I implore her with my eyes, but Mother doesn't see me. "Be a good child," she repeats. "I will leave Etsu with you, and the car will come to get you in the afternoon."

"But Mother..." Reverend Mother takes my hand. "Say goodbye to your mother, Theresa."

"Goodbye, Mother," I murmur, feeling like a marooned sheep. A sheep abandoned by her own mother...

When the car stopped in front of our high, tile-ridged gate, I slid out without waiting for Etsu, and began walking up the path between the trees. It was almost impossible to believe that everything was still there — the steppingstones placed at irregular intervals on the mossy ground, the shaggy rocks draped with red-black vines, the murmur of the hidden stream, and the sunshine spilling on the broad cycad leaves — and the peace and the quietness breathing in the shadow of the long, low eaves...

Etsu caught up with me as I was wandering off to the garden and whispered hurriedly, "Reiko Sama — you must go and say 'I am back' to your mother. She must be waiting anxiously for your return..."

I stood still for a minute, wondering. I didn't want to see Mother, I thought. I just couldn't face her now.

"Go away, Etsu."

"But Reiko Sama..."

"You don't have to tell her I'm back."

"But Reiko Sama..."

"I don't care..." I flung myself away from her and began running toward the house, leaving poor Etsu behind, still looking quite worried.

The parlor was quiet. The curtains were half drawn, and the air was cold. Only the little clock on the mantelpiece kept on ticking. No guests today, I thought with relief. I could have gone up to my room, but then I didn't want anybody to see me. I had a headache, and I wanted to be alone. I wanted a corner where I could hide — a corner where no one could ever find me — ever. I looked around, chose a big armchair in the far corner, curled myself up and closed my eyes.

Drops of tears came out, one by one, from between my tightly closed eyelids, rolled down my cheeks and stopped on my lips. They tasted oddly cold and salty — more salty and cold and bitter than the sea wind. I wish I could go back to Kamakura, I thought, dozing off. The sea looked always so happy and free — so free, even when it was angry, and the whole bay tossed with gray, biting waves...

Suddenly, someone snapped on the light, and I woke up, blinking at the sparkling chandelier above. Mother was standing in front of me, watching. "How do you do, Mother," I said, rubbing my eyes.

"We've looked all over for you," she said gently, smoothing my rumpled hair. "Really, you could have said something..."

"I was tired, Mother."

"Well, it's natural that you are tired, since this is

the first day. You should go to bed early tonight."

"But Mother, I am not going to school again, am I?"
The fear and the resentment came back in a flood, and
I felt my head begin to ache again, in a dull, throbbing
sort of way.

Mother looked at me, as if she was a bit surprised.
"But of course you are," she said determinedly. "Everyone has to go to school sooner or later."

"But Mother ... You said it was just because you've
promised..."

Mother sighed, pulling out a handkerchief from her
sleeve. "Really, since when have you become so stubborn — I thought you were such a nice, obedient
child..."

"Father said I didn't have to go," I insisted, even more
stubbornly. "He said if I studied very hard at home
then I didn't have to." But Mother interrupted me irritably. "Father and I decided that you should go."

"But Mother..." It can't be — Father couldn't have
gone back on his words. After all, he has promised...
"May I go and ask Father?" I stood up to go. But
Mother stopped me.

"Don't disturb him now, dear," she said with a frigid
patience. "Besides, it's no use asking — we have decided."

"But Mother..."

"Don't return words," ordered Mother shortly. And
for the first time in my life I saw her temper rising. A
thin blue vein appeared on her forehead, and she was
breathing hard as if to control herself. It bewildered and
frightened me, so I kept silent.

Turning away, Mother said, still angrily, "It's almost suppertime. You'd better go up and change."

"Reiko has gone on a hunger strike," reports my brother cheerfully from the opposite side of the supper table.

"She looks so funny with a long face. Just like the blowfish we used to catch at Kamakura," adds my sister with a smiling and cruel accuracy.

"Vous êtes fatiguée, n'est-ce pas?" says Mademoiselle Charlotte sympathetically. *"Pauvre petite..."*

The golden egg roll looks very soft and delicious, but I am not hungry. Very stubbornly I keep my eyes cast down, not touching any food.

"Sacred Heart you are entering, isn't it?" inquires my brother's tutor, gobbling a piece of tile fish. He is a student of the Imperial University, has a mop of hair and intent, philosophical eyes.

I nod again, without saying anything. Why do they have to keep on talking about it? I think to myself angrily. For some obscure reason I feel that if everyone stopped talking about my going to school, then Mother would forget about it entirely. But no one understands.

"Don't you want to go?" asks my brother indifferently. I look up quickly. Don't I want to go? As if no one knew that he too ran away on his first day at the kindergarten...

"It is a bit far," says Mademoiselle Charlotte. *"A son âge..."*

"If it's so far, then why can't you board at school?"

queried my brother's tutor. This is, as Mademoiselle Charlotte would say, *"le comble"* — and I can no longer keep back my tears. I look down at the table, and in spite of all my efforts, a big teardrop falls on the linen and makes a faint stain.

All this while Father and Mother have kept silence, which is, after all, not unusual. But tonight, there is something awkward in their silence. Or is it because I feel that way...I give a sidelong glance at Father. Sitting at the head of the table, he appears very preoccupied; also he carefully avoids looking in my direction. And as I watch him, my hurt feeling grows deeper. Father, whom I always thought so right, so fair...

Suddenly Father takes up his empty wineglass and tells Kiyo, "Pour some sherry for Reiko."

Mother raises her eyebrows, Mademoiselle Charlotte smiles, and my brother and my sister look at each other indignantly. Father turns to me imperturbably. "Drink it, Reiko," he says. "It will help you to get good sleep." But he still does not look me in the face.

The wine looks beautiful in the long-stemmed glass — heavy, golden, with a touch of amber spark in it. But I hang my head even lower, and push the crystal glass away. I can't possibly have anything from Father, I feel. The whole thing was, really, too painful...I push back my plate of fruits, slip down from the high-backed chair and murmur, "Please excuse me." Everyone looks at me in surprise. Why, what's wrong with her, their bewildered eyes say. Is she sick again? But I pay no attention to them. Almost running, I go out of the dining room, feeling the stare of everyone at my back. But I don't care. I hate all the grownups, I hate everyone, including even Mademoiselle Charlotte...

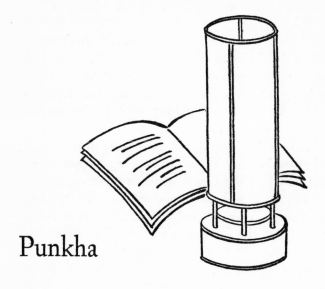

Punkha

FORGETFULNESS is a happy faculty. Of all things that are past, people tend to remember the more pleasant ones. And even if there are sad memories which keep on coming back, the sharpness of the sting is gone, the edge of the picture blurred, and you shrug your shoulders and say, "Oh well, it wasn't *so* bad after all . . ." Or am I wrong? *"Le passé est beaucoup plus doux que le présent,"* said Anatole France, *"et beaucoup plus sûr que l'avenir . . ."*

At any rate, that is how I think of my first days at school. I can no longer remember how sad I felt when my mother left me, stranded, so to speak, among strangers — foreigners, of all people. I shouldn't say, though, that I can't remember — for I do. What I meant to say is that I cannot *feel* the sorrow any longer. And there is a bit of difference. But on the whole, when I look back on the first three years of my school, I can say that they were happy ones. I look back, for instance, on those days I spent in the Pink Room with my classmates, reading, working with beads, and whispering to each other when Mother Welman's back was turned to us. I also remember the canary in the hanging cage above the window sill, and the picture of an English countryside on the wall, with green hills and meadows spreading quietly under the soft gray sky. The Pink Room and the canary are no longer there — one is burned down, and the school cat got the other. But the echo of the songs we used to sing, playing in the courtyard, keeps coming back. "The farmer in the dell, the farmer in the dell..." And "London bridge is falling down, falling down, falling down, London bridge is falling down, my fair lady," followed by the eternal refrain — "Children, be ladylike, be always ladylike..."

The convent school of the Sacred Heart of Jesus, where I spent thirteen years of my daytime life, had two sections. One was for the Japanese girls, starting from kindergarten and ending in the three-year course of normal school, and the other, much smaller, for the foreigners' children, with six junior grades, five senior classes, and one postgraduate year. Naturally, all the Japanese girls went to the Japanese school, unless they happened to be born abroad, or at least had spent part of their lives in foreign countries. And I still don't know why Father sent me — insisted, as a matter of fact against my mother's wish, that I should go to the Foreigners' Section.

But I have never questioned his motives — and never will. For I am, in a way, grateful for his choice. Even if the experience did bring a certain amount of confusion to my life, it still was a good thing, I imagine, that I had a chance to see a little bit of the Western world.

Not that I would go through my first few days at school again willingly. For I can still remember how utterly lost I felt, walking along the dark corridor with Reverend Mother, and how her long, black veil brushed across my cheek and left a faint trace of chill...As I think about it, the picture comes back, amazingly vivid and clear, although it happened almost two decades ago...

Two shadows in the hall, one tall and round, one small, scrawny, walking with hurried little steps to catch up with the other. Up the staircase and along the corridor the shadows move, till they come to a door at the end of it and stop. Reverend Mother, letting go my hand, flings back her veil and opens the door, without knocking.

The lesson is interrupted, and a small nun, sitting behind the teacher's desk, looks up. She is a slender, middle-aged person with an oval face and mild blue eyes.

"This is the new child, Mother Welman," says

Reverend Mother, pushing me forward. "The youngest of the Hatsumis," she adds unsmilingly.

"I see," replies Mother Welman, looking at me from top to toe. "There is a family likeness, isn't there?"

The room is small, sunny, and quite pink, with pictures of Our Lady and Infant Jesus on the wall, and in the corner, a big painted globe. There are geranium and fern pots on the window sill, and one, two, three — eight children sitting at their desks. They all glance at me, but without much curiosity.

"What is your name?" asks Mother Welman, taking my hand.

I keep silent, looking down at my toe. I have really two names — one Japanese, and one foreign, my baptismal name. It is difficult to decide which I should give...

"You do speak English, don't you dear?" asks Mother Welman, a trifle anxious. I shake my head in silence, because, really, I don't.

"Of course she does," replies Reverend Mother determinedly. "She is just a bit shy, that's all." Then after whispering something hurriedly to my new teacher she turns around to go. All the children stand up, make a curtsy and seat themselves again.

"Sit down, Theresa," says Mother Welman in a kind voice. "Florence, show her your book for today."

Florence has straight flaxen hair, large blue eyes, and rosy, smiling, mischievous lips. She pushes over her book across the desk, so that half of it lies on my side. But she doesn't say a word.

Mother Welman takes up her book, and the lesson goes on. I can understand a little English, but cannot read, write, or speak it, which makes things a bit difficult. So, sitting on the little pink chair, my hands on my lap, I gaze out of the window, getting a little sleepy.

But all of a sudden Mother Welman raises her voice. There is a slight commotion at the back row. "Gino," she calls. Then again, a little more decisively, "Gino Angelone."

A slender boy with curly black hair, in white sailor suit, stands up gingerly. "Yes, Mother."

"This is the third time I have to call your attention, Gino," says Mother Welman, a bit sternly. "Would you kindly tell us what you have been doing under your desk?"

"Nothing, Mother." Gino looks up very innocently, his dark green eyes blinking under the long black lashes.

Mother sighs. "Very well, Gino. Would you please recite the first four lines of 'Admirals all, for England's sake'?"

"Admirals all, for England's sake..." The little boy begins rapidly, stops, and looks up at the ceiling as if he can find the rest of the poem there.

"Go on, dear," encourages Mother Welman.

"Er — For England's sake — For England's sake..." Gino falters, flushing a little.

Mother Welman gives up. "That will do, Gino. You haven't done your homework again. Go up to the blackboard, and write it out three times."

Gino takes his book and goes up to the blackboard,

still looking very innocent. But on his way he pauses beside a dark-complexioned girl to pull her long black braided hair. The girl slaps away his hand, irritably.

"Be a gentleman, Gino," commands Mother Welman, then to the little girl with defiant eyes, "Koblab, you too — you should be lady enough not to behave that way . . ." At my back a pair of twins — pretty, blue-eyed, with long blond curls, looking like a pair of identical dolls — whisper to each other, giggling under their breath.

Finally the bell rings somewhere far away, and Mother Welman closes her book. The children stand up, say a short prayer and file out silently into the corridor.

I am left in the room, feeling lonely. But I don't want to follow the children, for I am shy and afraid. I'll go find Etsu, I think to myself. Then I can sit and wait with her till the car comes. Quietly I slip out of the little pink room and walk down the corridor.

The long, narrow hall is very dark, so dark that I can hardly see anything. But at the far end of it a glass-paneled swinging door shines faintly. Perhaps, I think, there is a gateway behind that door — perhaps I can find Etsu in the garden.

I push open the door and go out. But no — there is no garden or even a gateway. Instead there lies another stretch of corridor, long, gray, softly lighted and quiet. I stand still for a while, wondering what to do. Then suddenly a hand grasps my arm and I am jerked back the way I came. Quite bewildered, I follow this new apparition obediently. Once outside, it begins talking in a rapid, animated fashion, pointing toward the door. I look up in amazement. Apparently I am being scolded for something — what precisely, is not certain however. Words like "convent," "cloistered," "rules," "community" come into my ears, but all in all they do not convey any meaning. The scolding person is very tall, has a fierce red face and gleaming, fiery eyes. Although I don't understand what I am being scolded about, she keeps on gripping my arm so tight that it is all I can do not to burst out crying...

So I began my first day at school, but soon I became used to the new environment. I learned to speak English, and began to make friends. There were Florence from Switzerland, Gino Angelone from Rome, Sylvia and Cynthia, the American twins, Koblab Sompatisiri, daughter of the mayor of Bangkok, Kulsum and Sherin Ismail from Cairo, Hideko, whose father was an ambassador to Sweden, and Josephine Dodds, with long, beautiful golden hair. Together we played and studied in the sunny pink room, while the canary twittered in its cage, and the cat went trotting by underneath the ivy-covered window, and Mother Rose, our aged sewing mistress, dozed off into a nap.

It was very different from the life I led at home, but I liked it. For the first time I learned rhymes from Mother Goose, and met Jack and the Beanstalk in my arithmetic book. How fascinating those books were — with little English girls and English boys, lambs, retrievers and sailing boats, and when you pressed your

nose deep in between the pages there was a faint smell
of newly bound paper, a smell just like that of a fresh
green banana...And there was the morning excursion
to the flower bed, with picks and shovels and watering
cans, to plant roses and nasturtiums — and then the Friday afternoon Benediction, with incense, jeweled
monstrance glistening in the shadow, and the wave of
Gregorian chant floating up to the high, arched
ceiling...

But there was, I think, one thing that disconcerted
my teachers at school — I was too quiet. Other children
had much more spirit. They spoke freely, even boldly
to the Mothers. They asked questions without being
prompted, and answered unhesitatingly when spoken
to. But whenever someone asked me a question I felt
my throat tighten, and nothing but "Yes Mother," or
"No Mother" would come out — and sometimes not even
that.

But I couldn't help it — at home I was taught to be
quiet, obedient, and not to speak unless spoken to by the
elders. For a Japanese girl should be shy and modest,
said my mother, and if it was good to possess many
virtues, it was even a greater virtue to conceal them.
And above all, never, never should a woman flaunt her
knowledge...So I remained silent and unresponsive
throughout my first term, and was consequently branded
as being "rather backward."

Not that I minded it at all. On the contrary, I enjoyed
the reputation. People, especially the religious, harbor
an infinite amount of patience and long-suffering love

for those who are so unfortunately not quite up to par.
And I, being classified as one whose motion was slow,
and whose comprehension even slower, enjoyed an
almost unlimited indulgence.

So the first year went by, and I graduated from the
Pink Room to the Blue Room, while my class dwindled,
augmented, and dwindled again, as each foreign family
sailed from Yokohama and a new one sailed in. Although
I was promoted to the second junior grade, the substance
of my lessons remained more or less the same, and if it
hadn't been for Mother Rose and my stupid Punkha, the
Negro doll, I would have gone on my happily inarticulate
ways undisturbed during my second year. But then I
didn't know — that sooner or later I had to learn to
adjust myself, between the two different lives, between
school and home, between East and West, and that what
was esteemed in one was not necessarily so in the
other...

It was Bishop Walsh who gave me the toy. He was on
a brief visit from America on some mission, and brought
the little black doll in the corner of his steamer trunk.
One evening after dinner he took it out from his cassock
pocket, said "Here," and gave it to me. I blinked. It was
the first time I had seen a black doll — a little colored boy
squatting, his legs crossed, with a slice of watermelon
in his hands. But the most interesting part was that
when you pressed a button at his back, the two black
hands went up to his mouth with the slice of watermelon,
and the boy took a large bite out of it, or so it almost
seemed.

"Thank you, Father," I said, hurrying away to show it to Etsu.

But her reaction was negative. "It's black, Reiko Sama," she said, almost gasping. She came from a country where all the women had silken white skin, and were taught not to spoil it.

"But that's why I like it," I insisted. "After all, aren't the Ainus black too?"

"Why no, Reiko Sama," protested Etsu, with an injured local patriotism. "They are not black. They are just hairy, that's all, and a little tattooed..."

The next day I took the toy to school. And of course it caused a sensation.

"Say, that's awfully clever," said Martin, just arrived from England. "He's an Indian, isn't he?"

"No he isn't," corrected Florence, peering on tiptoe over his shoulder. "He's a Negro—I've seen them at Marseille."

"Oh?" said Martin, not quite convinced. "But my uncle brought home someone just like that from Bombay last year."

"I've seen them in Paris too," said Florence, tossing her head. "My father told me they were from Africa."

"I don't like watermelon," said Gino, looking at the doll contemptuously. "I'd much rather have *tempura* or a chicken pie."

Kulsum and Sherin Ismail stood apart, hand in hand, uninterested and silent.

After due discussion, it was decided that no matter what race the doll belonged to, there were few black dolls, and so it was quite a distinguished one. It was named Punkha, and I kept it on my desk, very kindly, for everyone to see for the next few days. Then of course after a while general interest waned, and the black boy became a fixture on my desk, just like my inkpot and the pencil holder, and no one paid attention to it any longer.

Then one morning something unexpected happened. It was Monday, shortly before Christmas. As soon as we said our prayers and sat down, Mother Rose put on her glasses and announced that she was going to collect a donation for the poor. "As I told you last week, anything for the poor — books, clothing, toys. I hope you haven't forgotten them."

I had forgotten it. Or rather, I had never heard about it. Most likely I was, as usual, looking out of the window, dreaming about something else when she told us about it. But apparently the rest of my classmates remembered to bring something. The drawers and satchels were opened, and soon all sorts of little items appeared on their desks. Dear me, I thought in panic. What could I give? I had nothing with me.

After a while Mother Rose stopped in front of my desk, carrying a large basket already half filled on her arm. "And you, Theresa?" she asked, blinking at me inquiringly through her glasses. I kept silence, looking up at Mother Rose with helpless eyes, feeling trapped. But, I suppose, she was used to my unresponsiveness. She looked down at my desk, and her glance fell on my Negro doll. "Oh, this is your donation, is it dear?"

she said, nodded approval, brushed it into her basket, and went on.

I sat there feeling miserable. It wasn't that I missed the doll. I wasn't really interested in it anymore. But what if Bishop Walsh asked me, as he once did, "How's the little Negro boy doing?" What could I say then? It wasn't good manners to give away things received as gifts from someone else. And Mother might scold me, both for not paying attention in class and for being so uncourteous to our guest.

Actually I would have forgotten about the doll within a few days, and Bishop Walsh never came back to Japan to ask about it. So everything might have gone well, if only Gerda didn't come in to borrow a ruler from me that afternoon. Gerda was one class above me. She had sharp, inquisitive brown eyes and an upturned nose, was inclined to be a little bossy, and I never liked her too well. "What did you do with Punkha?" she asked, noticing the absence of the doll from my desk. "Did you finally take it home?"

"No," I said, still feeling rather unhappy. "I had to give it up."

"For the poor?"

"Yes."

"Why are you making such a long face then?"

"I didn't want to."

"Why?"

"Because — someone gave it to me."

Gerda shrugged her shoulders as if to say "So what?" and went away. And I thought no more about it.

But the next day I was summoned by Mother Rose during the noon recreation. It was Gerda who came to call me.

"Why does she want to see me?" I asked, suddenly frightened.

"I don't know," said Gerda, smiling maliciously. "You better go right now — she's waiting for you in the linen room."

Slowly, reluctantly, I went up the stairs to the linen room. Did Gerda say anything to Mother Rose? I wondered. But what could she say — I didn't really tell her anything...

Mother Rose was sitting in the corner of the linen room, bending over a piece of darning cloth. I stood at the doorway, watching her in silence, all the time my heart beating faster. Finally she looked up, noticed me standing on the threshold, and motioned me to her side. I went in, dragging my feet, going around the table very slowly.

Mother Rose placed her piece of darning on the table and took my hands in hers. "Theresa dear," she said, her lips trembling a little. "I heard you didn't want to give up your doll yesterday. Why didn't you say so, dear?" Her small, red-rimmed eyes blinked at me a little sadly. "You should have told me..." she repeated, shaking her head.

I kept silence, staring down at the table. What could I say — I couldn't utter a word even if I had wanted to. I was tongue-tied, and I couldn't help it.

"Why didn't you say so?" inquired Mother Rose again,

in a puzzled tone. Then she opened a drawer of her sewing table, took out my little Punkha and quietly placed it in my hand. "You should be more explicit, dear," she murmured, turning away, and for a moment, a look of — was it disappointment? — crossed her wrinkled gray face. "You may go, dear," she said, taking up her sewing again.

Mother sent the car to pick me up that day, and on the way home, passing through the wild patch of ground near the school-gate, I took Punkha out from my satchel and looked at it again. The little black doll didn't look humorous and good-natured anymore. It seemed to bear a grin — a hideous little grin on his shiny black face. And as I gazed at it, I began to feel ill.

Quietly, I opened the car window and threw the doll away, aiming as far as I could into the deep tangle of brushes. But as I watched Punkha go off into the air, making a black curve in the sunshine then down into the shaggy undergrowth — even then I thought I saw him bending over his slice of watermelon, grinning mockingly...

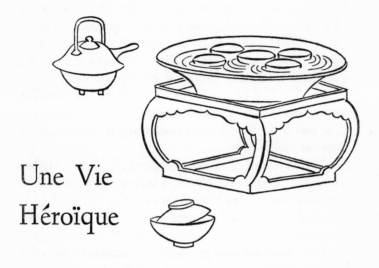

Une Vie Héroïque

"Whom shall we have for the tea?" asked Mother, absently biting the tip of her new writing brush. There were stacks of paper on her desk — opaque Chinese scrolls, gilt-edged invitation cards, long white envelopes — and Mother looked down at them a little wearily.

"Anyone, Mother." After all, it wasn't my idea — to have a birthday party for Mademoiselle Charlotte. All grown-up parties were as a rule frightfully boring. And how did Mother know that Mademoiselle Charlotte wanted one anyway?

Mother put down her brush with a sigh. "It's really

so much bother," she murmured. "I'm almost tempted to let it go. But after all, we should do something..."

Lying on the matted floor beside Mother's sitting cushion, and playing with Tama's newborn kitten I kept silent. For I knew it wasn't exactly a birthday party that Mother was giving—it happened to be, actually, a farewell gathering for Mademoiselle Charlotte. She had been with us for more than a year, but now that I was going to school, and what with the increasing homework in English, really no use cluttering up the child's mind...

"What about Fräulein Roggendorff?" said Mother brightly. "She speaks French, I believe. Don't you think it would be nice to have them meet?"

"But Mother..." I raised myself on my elbow, startled. Mademoiselle Charlotte and Fräulein Roggendorff—could any two persons be so different from each other? Why, it would be like putting anemone with a potted dwarf pine...

But Mother didn't pay any attention to me. "Well then, Fräulein Roggendorff," said she, addressing one more envelope with a sigh.

I hadn't seen Fräulein Roggendorff for quite some time, now that she no longer gave me piano lessons, and my German doll, her namesake, lay in the dark corner of my nursery long since forgotten. It wouldn't be, however, quite accurate to say that I hadn't seen her— for it was really a question of *her* not seeing me...

Oh, we met often enough—as a matter of fact, every Sunday at church, and that was what seemed to me so strange. No matter what church I went to, no matter at what time, there was Fräulein Roggendorff, kneeling in the front pew, her face buried in her large, bony, ash-colored hands, deep in prayer.

Why did she pray so often, and so long? And why did her shoulders, clad in a coarse woolen jacket, sag so much as if under a heavy load? And why did the light that flickered in from the high stained-glass windows shine so pale and lifeless on her bent shaggy head?

Perhaps, I thought, perhaps a long time ago, long before I was born, Fräulein Roggendorff was on this earth. And she committed a mortal sin. What exactly it was no one knows, but some horrible crime which could not be atoned for in a lifetime. And Our Lord had ordered her to attend a thousand — or ten thousand — masses on this earth, before she would be permitted to enter his Kingdom. And that is why she was here now... I could picture her in a silent, secret, determined pilgrimage, from church to church, from devotion to devotion, leaving unseen after the last Gospel, and flying on her large broomstick over the city of Tokyo, in search of another mass she could attend...

Of course I never told my fancies to anyone — not for a long time. One had to be careful about mentioning such things. But nevertheless when I sat next to Mademoiselle Charlotte in the church, and she looked, during the long sermon of Père Flaujacque, a bit dreamy and preoccupied, I felt an irresistible longing to pull her sleeve and point at the kneeling figure of Fräulein Roggendorff in front, and tell her what I knew...

And I did tell her once, on the way home from church. But Mademoiselle Charlotte didn't appreciate my theory at all. "Thérèse," she sounded shocked, "you shouldn't say such things about other people..." But then she turned away, I think, to hide her smile.

Too bad I told her, I thought, still lying on the matted floor, teasing the little kitten with a branch of goat-willow. Not that I mistrusted Mademoiselle Charlotte — but one never knew ... Grownups as a rule weren't very good at keeping secrets. And now that she was to meet Fräulein Roggendorff — did she still remember about her punishment and the broomstick? Heavens, I hoped not...

The bamboo outside the corridor rustled in the wind, and shadows began to deepen on the matted floor. The tiny cream-colored kitten made a snatch at the goat-willow, missed, and looked up, bewildered.

"This is all," said Mother, gathering up the white oblong envelopes. "And remember not to say anything to Mademoiselle Charlotte till the day comes — for I'm going to tell her it's just a tea..."

Sunshine danced on the pomegranate tree. It danced on Mother's jade hairpins, and slid down on my embroidered sleeves. It danced on the smooth brown hair of Mademoiselle Charlotte, and stopped on her tiny pearl and silver brooch.

"Mes félicitations, chère Mademoiselle Charlotte."

"Merci, ma petite Thérèse." Mademoiselle Charlotte

stood, flushed and smiling in front of her birthday cake. It had just been brought in — a tall layer cake all draped in pink and white froth, with tiny silver bubbles and blue roses on the top.

"Mais, que c'est joli..." Mademoiselle Charlotte bent down over the table, admiring. And the guests, moving across the lawn in groups, like huge bouquets of flowers swept gently by the breeze, looked at each other and smiled.

The weather was perfect. Sunshine poured over the lawn, light, sparkling, with an almost unnoticeable touch of chilliness. Above us the sky stretched, high and mild, veiled with golden-blue autumn haze. Tables were laden with cakes, flowers and fruit — shining brown chestnuts, persimmons, juicy white peaches and purple-black grapes. And around them stood ladies in silk kimonos, laughing and gossiping behind their fans, their white handkerchiefs fluttering in the breeze...

"Won't you cut the cake, Mademoiselle Charlotte?"

"Oh, yes, of course..."

Mother handed her a long carved ivory knife, and Mademoiselle Charlotte began cutting the cake, carefully.

"Here, Thérèse. Please take this to the lady sitting near the flower bed. *Cette dame en habit brun...*"

The lady in brown near the flower bed? Oh, yes, Fräulein Roggendorff, alone, as usual, and silent, sitting next to the cluster of burning amaranths like a gray pebble cast off and forgotten by someone...

Through the fluttering silk sleeves and the scent of

perfume I tiptoed my way to the Fräulein, balancing the tea and cake tray in my hands.

"How do you do, Fräulein Roggendorff."

"Ah, how do you do, Fräulein Reiko," replied my piano teacher, looking up. Horn-rimmed spectacles, black leather boots, brown serge suit and her hair as stringy as ever. But today she had a pair of gloves on, and a brown felt hat that sagged a little. "You have grown taller, haven't you, Fräulein Reiko? Of course it has been quite a while since I saw you last."

"Yes, Fräulein Roggendorff." Good thing — the broomstick wasn't apparently mentioned...

"And how is your piano?" inquired the Fräulein as I handed her the dish of birthday cake and a teacup. "Have you been practicing regularly?"

"No..." I faltered. Somehow I felt I shouldn't say I had neglected it completely of late. "School keeps me so busy now..."

"Too bad." Fräulein sounded quite sad — really disheartened. "Too bad — you were doing so nicely before."

I kept silent. It was awkward, standing in front of Fräulein Roggendorff not knowing what to say, as if I were called to the teachers' room at school for some scolding or other. I wish I could go away, I thought to myself. But no — that would be impolite...

So I selected a little porcelain stool near the flower bed and sat down, gathering up my sleeves carefully on my knees. For a while we sat without a word, while Fräulein Roggendorff took up a spoon and began stirring her tea. Somewhere a cicada was singing its early autumn song, and a bird whisked through the gold-powdered sky. Above our heads, the tall *mandala* tree murmured, and beside me the chrysanthemums nodded, their brocaded petals heavy with dew. From time to time wind brought snatches of conversation across the lawn.

"And my dear, did you hear what the old baroness said to the bride-to-be?"

"Heavens, it hardly seems worth a title, with such a mother-in-law..."

Tinkling laughter, silvery and cold, and embroidered kimonos shining in the sun.

Suddenly Fräulein Roggendorff looked up and remarked, "She looks gay — that lady. Mademoiselle Charlotte."

I looked up too. There on the other side of the garden stood Mademoiselle Charlotte, talking and laughing with Mother, her hands flung out, looking helplessly amused at something.

"Yes," I agreed. "She is a French lady."

Without saying anything more, Fräulein Roggendorff took up the spoon and began stirring her tea again. The small silver tongue slid quietly into the amber-colored liquid and went around and around — but no more bubbles came up from the bottom of the cup. The tea must have gotten cold...

That was how the two foreign ladies met, and at first I don't think they liked each other. To me, it seemed perfectly natural that they didn't. Why should they? They were so different from each other... And that is why it came as a surprise when Mademoiselle Charlotte announced that upon leaving our home she intended living with Fräulein Roggendorff.

"But are you sure you want to?" asked Mother a bit doubtfully. "After all, you are welcome to stay with us as long as you wish..."

Mother had extended the invitation many times, not that she expected Mademoiselle Charlotte to accept it...And of course she didn't.

"Thank you, Mrs. Hatsumi, but all the same," Mademoiselle Charlotte would say with a little smile, "I intend to teach at St. Maule, and it would be more convenient if I lived nearer downtown..."

So she went to live with Fräulein Roggendorff in a little house on the Persimmon Tree Slope, and with great difficulty I wangled permission from Mother to go and visit her every week. It wasn't for my French, however. It was my embroidery that Mother wanted me to continue, French embroidery being, at the time, quite a fashionable thing for young girls to learn.

Every Friday, on the way home from school I took a bus to the Persimmon Tree Slope, to the little wooden house perched on the incline, standing on tiptoe. It was an old building, two-storied on one side, three on the other, with very little sunshine and a lot of dampness. The parlor always smelled musty — the smell of dried-up inkpots, dusty windowpanes, withered furniture and worn-out carpet. An equally old withered woman and her husband kept the house for them.

Mademoiselle Charlotte always welcomed me warmly.

"*Ah, bonjour Thérèse — ça va bien?*" she would say, her face beaming with a big smile. Then, "*Entrez, entrez, asseyez-vous,*" stepping lightly back to her room and pulling up a chair for me. And always, after the lesson, we had tea with light little biscuits. Mademoiselle Charlotte was very fond of pastries, but then I think they made her a little homesick. "Nothing like the ones we used to have at home," she would say, shaking her head sadly at the tiny cream puffs. "*C'est pas mal — ces choux à la crême — mais quand même...*" And a momentary mist would pass her eyes as she gazed away. What was she thinking about then — her home? Her home with its flowering orange trees and the sun, strong, warm and enveloping, pouring over the white sand and the sparkling indigo sea?

But then, outside our window lay the garden, with leafless trees and the winter-bitten shrubs, and the wind — cold, invisible — that went circling, circling, gathering up the brown leaves and blowing them away...

Sometimes Fräulein Roggendorff opened the door for me, much to my discomfort. For some reason she continued to frighten me, long after I had grown up. I felt uneasy — especially when she stared at me through her glasses and asked, "Ah well, Fräulein Reiko, are you still practicing the piano?"

Hesitantly I would answer, "Well — from time to time..." in a tone that could be taken for either yes or no. Really, I couldn't tell her I was taking lessons from someone else — Nadia Wradimirskaya at Sacred Heart, because Mother thought it would be "more convenient."

Nadia was a lot different from Fräulein Roggendorff. She was temperamental. She would give me an extremely easy piece one week, and then an almost impossible one the next. But all in all Nadia was an easier teacher to deal with — she wasn't so fussy about phrasings and counterpoints, and didn't expect as much work and precision as Fräulein Roggendorff did.

No — the trouble was that somehow I felt she knew... Fräulein Roggendorff knew that I was taking piano lessons from someone else. But she never said anything.

I think it was Fräulein Roggendorff's love of method and precision that drove Mademoiselle Charlotte almost to distraction at times. Very often, when we were sitting in the study, Fräulein Roggendorff's pupil came, and across the corridor the piano lesson began. For a while Mademoiselle Charlotte would keep on sitting without, seemingly, paying any attention to the noise. Then she would begin to fidget on her chair. And as if to drown the sound of the piano, she would start talking to me, very rapidly, about her home, her country, her childhood, her mother... After a few minutes she would drop her hands on her lap, gazing up at the ceiling with despair in her eyes. "Really, I don't mind music — I adore it. I don't mind Bach — Bach — Bach. But it's the constant repetition! *Ein, zwei, drei...*" Then she would say in an imploring tone, "Thérèse, would you mind *very* much going and closing the door?"

It was an unpleasant task, to go and close Fräulein Roggendorff's door under her nose, while she was giving her lesson. But there was nothing I could do to get out of it. I would stand up reluctantly, walk across the corridor on tiptoe, and begin, very gently, to close the door, hoping to heaven she wouldn't notice what I was about. But most invariably she did notice it. Abruptly her counting would stop, and she would turn around, giving me a cold, fierce look through her spectacles. But she never said anything. Not a word.

Although Fräulein Roggendorff was a very conspicuous figure among the foreigners in Tokyo, no one knew very much about her. Not even, I think, Mademoiselle Charlotte. They said she was quite a scholar — degrees from various European universities, in music, in philosophy, in classical languages, and heaven knows what. But why she came to the Orient, and why she stayed remained a mystery. Life in Tokyo was too transient, too impersonal, for anyone to take the trouble of speculating on such problems, and the Fräulein continued, making her solemn rounds teaching German and piano, in her age-old flannel jacket, her boots, and with her brown, weather-beaten portfolio. Nothing seemed to touch her — not even loneliness.

Nothing, that was, except illness. For one cold day that winter, shortly after the first snow fell in Tokyo, Fräulein Roggendorff went to bed with a cold. Several days later she was taken to the Angel's Hospital, and for weeks the little house on the Persimmon Tree Slope remained very quiet.

It was a bit difficult for me at the time to imagine

Fräulein Roggendorff as a patient. A patient lying in a hospital bed, between white sheets... People like her, I felt, couldn't be sick — not at least seriously. She seemed too sturdy, too eternal, almost that Death itself would be afraid — I could picture Death dressed in flowing black, looking pale, and stepping aside to let the Fräulein pass, bowing politely over his sleeves...

But I was mistaken, sadly and seriously. And it was little Jules who told me about the death of Fräulein Roggendorff. Jules, six-year-old son of Madame la Comtesse de Frigidaire — her real name I have forgotten, a lady so incredibly cool, elegant, and haughty — was also a piano pupil of Fräulein Roggendorff.

"You know, she's dead," shouted Jules, running up to me one day in the school playground. "I don't have to practice the piano anymore!"

"Who?" I asked, taken by surprise.

"Fräulein Roggendorff. Mother said she had neu-mo-nia."

"Oh?" I said. Somehow it sounded unbelievable.

"And you know," continued Jules. "You know what I heard?"

"No," I said, feeling a bit annoyed. How should I know — little boys could be, at times, such a bother...

"I heard my nanny tell my mother this morning," whispered Jules, his blue eyes getting larger and larger. "Do you know why Fräulein Roggendorff came to Japan?"

"No."

"Nanny said Fräulein Roggendorff came to Japan

because of a pro-fe-ssor," said Jules, as if reciting a poem he memorized. "A Japanese pro-fe-ssor. She was in-lovit him, but he was married."

"Oh, no," I gasped. The whole idea was so hideously fantastic. Fräulein Roggendorff and a man...

"But it's true," protested Jules with an injured dignity. "I heard my nanny say so."

"But Jules..." I looked at him standing there in his immaculately cut sailor suit, hands in his pockets, and sunshine stopping on his curly brown hair. "But Jules," I said slowly, "you shouldn't say such things about — dead people..."

"Why?" The innocent blue eyes looked up, puzzled. Why? I didn't know either — not really ...

"This is very nice of you, and your mother," said the young Franciscan nun, taking up the bunch of white carnations from my arms. "We will place them in the chapel for the Requiem Mass tomorrow. And now, perhaps you would like to say a prayer for the departed, yes?"

Down we went through the long, silent corridor, down flights of stairs and along the narrow, lightless passage. It was very quiet, there in the hospital basement, and the sound of my lacquered sandals fell softly on the floor, echoing on the walls. Finally we came to a closed door, where the nun stopped. And with a quick, light movement she turned around, placing her hand on the knob.

"This is the room," she whispered, turning the knob very gently as if she didn't want to disturb someone.

But Mother said "in the chapel" I thought, panic-stricken. She certainly didn't tell me "death chamber." What was I going to do now? I stood on the threshold, carefully averting my eyes. If only I could explain that I had never seen a dead person, and I was afraid...

"Come in," said the nun, still whispering. Reluctantly I raised my eyes and stepped into the room. It was dark, except for the thin rays of light that filtered in from the high, small window. At the head of the bed, two candles burned softly on a white-cloth-covered stand, throwing orange-colored shadow on the black and silver cross, and beside them a bunch of violets draped on the edge of a small crystal vase. A faint smell of camphor clung in the air, and on the bed — or was it a coffin? — lay Fräulein Roggendorff, very quiet and still, her wax-pale hands clasped on her bosom, looking much smaller than she used to be.

The nun dipped her fingers in the holy-water vessel, made a sign of the cross and knelt down. I followed mechanically, now unable to take my eyes off the face that looked so still. So this was death — it wasn't at all frightening, really. It was like someone asleep...

The candle sputtered, throwing a trembling light over the silver-gray hair and the chiseled forehead of Fräulein Roggendorff. And in the twilight gloom the cluster of violets drooped heavily, whispering...

So this is the end of her pilgrimage, I thought, settling down in the car. She had finished her thousand — or was it ten thousand? — masses, and there was going to be another one tomorrow, said for *her*, this time. But still, I couldn't quite see why she needed any more prayers. Didn't she pray enough for her own salvation? More than enough?

"Mais, certainement," said Mademoiselle Charlotte. *"Elle a prié pour tout le monde..."*

We were walking along the avenue, on our way up to the foreign cemetery in Yokohama. It was a lovely day in May — warm, tranquil and sleepy. All along the road plane trees shook their boughs, casting jade-green shadows on the paved sidewalk. From time to time a car went by, gliding along the avenue noiselessly, swiftly, shining like a black beetle, then disappearing into the clear torrent of sun.

"She had suffered very much," said Mademoiselle Charlotte, panting a little. "But she never told me. She never told anyone."

The road became uphill, and the sun a little warmer, a little brighter. But the houses behind the hedges, stood still and quiet, cool under the shadow of the trees. We walked past the brick buildings of Saint Joseph's School, past the white wall of the General Hospital, and finally came to the cemetery, on the edge of a slope, overlooking the bay.

We went through the tall iron gate, and down the path through rows of passanias. On both sides were graves — stone monuments of different shape and size, with inscription in all languages — Latin, English,

Italian, French, German, and on one of them, a little marble angel stood with a wreath in his hand.

"*Voilà*," said Mademoiselle Charlotte, looking at the little enclosure with a round-topped tombstone. IN MEMORIAM — ANNA ROGGENDORFF — REQUIESCAT IN PACE — then the dates of birth and death.

We changed the flowers in the stone vase, said a little prayer, and then sat down on the grassy steps that led up to the tomb. The sky was warm and dazzling, and the sunshine lay dozing, over the soft green hillside, over the red and blue shingles of foreign homes, and over the slanting thatched roofs of farming cottages half buried in the trees. And far below, the bay shimmered, blue, tranquil and sunny.

"Look, Thérèse," said Mademoiselle Charlotte, pointing downward. "It looks exactly like the one I came on."

A white, slender two-masted ship, graceful as a sea gull, passed slowly by, on its way out from the harbor, leaving a long, sparkling line of wave behind. And then a little pilot boat, like a busy water spider, skimming ahead of a huge, black, red-masted ocean liner, coming in from the sea.

"It must be a French boat," decided Mademoiselle Charlotte. "Looks so much like the one I knew..."

"Will you be going home?" I asked softly.

Mademoiselle Charlotte shrugged her shoulders. "I don't know — perhaps." Then she smiled. "When you are away so long..." She broke off, and looked down toward the sea again. There was something a bit dry, a bit odd, in her smile. "When you are away so long," she repeated gently. "You can't go back — very easily. So you stay."

"You mean, you can't go back home anymore?"

"Go back anywhere, Thérèse..."

I shook my head, unable to understand. Didn't she have a home, a family, relatives and friends? Why couldn't she go back?...

"Anna was an extraordinary person," said Mademoi-selle Charlotte, standing up. She looked suddenly old, and a little tired. "Sometimes, I think she didn't — quite belong to this world... Shall we go, Thérèse?"

"*Mais oui, mademoiselle.*" But I was still puzzled, following her up the stairs.

Under the *passania* trees the little white angel stood, one hand on the pillar, one hand holding a wreath, looking down toward the sea with his round, unseeing eyes, following the white ship that went sailing — sailing beyond the gossamer horizon to the unknown ports of the world ...

When the Spirits
Conflict

"So you are not coming back, Theresa?" said Mother Welman, gathering me to her knees. "You won't forget us, will you dear?"

"No, Mother." I felt uncomfortable, leaning on her lap, with the cool softness of her veil brushing against my cheek. It was the last day at school. The graduation ceremony had finished hours ago, and down the corridor, up the stairs, came the noise of the boarders going home. Sound of hurried footsteps, luggage being dragged across the hall, echoes of distant laughter, and "Don't forget to write, Regina, you have my address in Bangkok?" followed by Regina's high-pitched voice, fading down the hallway, "No, I won't. Goodbye, *bon voyage*..." Then somebody wailing, *"Whatever* happened to Spider? I have to take her to the station with me *this* minute..."

Outside the window the loquat trees rustled in the early summer breeze. Somewhere, a horn sounded, then there was silence. Already the quiet, sleepy holiday air hung over the school, in the shadowy corners of the room, on the dusty desks and chairs.

"We'll miss you, Theresa," repeated Mother Welman. I kept silence. I could have told her I'd miss her too — but somehow I didn't.

"Of course we'll miss you," said Mother Brady, rushing into the room. "Come and say goodbye to me, Theresa." Again I was enveloped in the black veil. Mother Welman sighed and looked out the window.

"Don't forget you will always be one of *our* children," said Mother Brady, releasing me. Then remembering her errand she added, "Your mother is waiting for you, Theresa — she is in the parlor with Reverend Mother."

Down in the cloak room, Sister Casey, as grumpy and formidable as ever, waited for me to come and get my hat. "Hurry, hurry, child," she called, spotting me at the end of the corridor and rattling her keys. "All afternoon I've been waiting to lock the door — one would think I had the whole day..."

I ran into the cloakroom, brushing past the tall figure of Sister Casey, found my hat and dashed out of the door, panting. "Goodbye, Sister."

"Goodbye, dear," said Sister Casey indifferently, pinning a bunch of keys to her blue cotton apron.

I was all ready to walk away, but something stopped me. I turned around. "You know, I'm not coming back next term," I said.

Sister Casey looked up, incredulous. "Not coming back? What for, child?" she demanded, coming a step forward. "Are you going abroad?"

"No. I'm going to change, to Japanese School," I answered, backing away toward the stairs.

"Hum," said the Sister, narrowing her eyes. "Japanese School — whatever for?" Then in a tone of gruff contempt, "There are too many children there, I tell you. You will be — regimented."

I shrugged my shoulders. Anyway what could I do about it? It certainly wasn't my idea to start with . . . "Well, goodbye, Sister," I said, half turning to go up the stairs.

"Goodbye, dear," said Sister Casey. And for the first time since I'd known her, a smile — a reluctant, struggling sort of smile — went across her face. "Come back to see us often, will you?"

"Yes, Sister." One hand on the railing, I watched her back receding toward the convent door, tall and majestic, still shaking her head as if to say, "Hum, Japanese School — whatever for?"

There was no summer holiday for me that year. Everyone else went away — my sisters to the sea, my brothers to the mountains, but I stayed with Mother, in the boiling heat of Tokyo. "You are so behind in everything Japanese," said she, leafing through the first and second grade textbooks. "You will have a lot of trouble catching up."

So our studies began, and my days became full. Soon I went through the first-, second-, and third-year textbooks, and Mother produced more of them from the cellar — moth-eaten, hand-bound books, the ones she had used when she was small.

"I think, Mrs. Hatsumi," objected one of my tutors mildly, "the standard you set is a bit too high for the third grade..." He happened to be a primary-school teacher himself.

"But when I was young," countered Mother, "we had to learn things far more difficult. Why, I'd learned by heart the *Analects* long before Reiko's age." Then turning to me she added, "Besides, it's your fundamentals that I am afraid of — you can't learn just everything from school texts..."

So the lessons on my fundamentals went on — national language and history, geography and arithmetic, hourlong brush writing and classical Chinese, the language of the learned. Even now I sadly remember those mornings spent in my mother's room, with a book of Confucius on her desk, and my voice faltering after each word as she pointed to them one by one with a long ivory stick. Then the long afternoons while the lawn sizzled under the midsummer sun, and cicadas clamored in the paulownia trees just outside the window and I waited for the three o'clock tea to be brought in and the lessons to be over.

Gradually the heat floated away. The azure sky became deeper. The large, trembling leaves of the Chinese hawthorn became fringed light yellow, and a touch of chill crept into the evening breeze. Toward the middle of September my new term at the Japanese School began.

We arrived a little late the first day, and were greeted by Madame Hirata, the dean. "Well, well," she said, nodding at my mother from the stone steps of the entrance hall. "How do you do, Mrs. Hatsumi. So glad you came at last. The classes have started, however. Would you like to sit through one of them, Mrs. Hatsumi?"

"Oh, may I?" said Mother. "Reiko is so behind in everything, I am a little afraid..."

"I am sure there won't be any trouble," interrupted Madame Hirata. "There is nothing very difficult in the third-grade course — but I *am* glad, Mrs. Hatsumi, that you didn't make your decision any later. I have all the admiration for the good Mothers' training, but after all, a Japanese girl should be educated in a Japanese school. Don't you think so, Mrs. Hatsumi? It's really a matter of the right spirit..."

Looking at her broad, pickled-plum face, graying hair swept back in a bun, and the complacent half-smile above her striped silk kimono, I decided, somehow or other, that I didn't like Madame Hirata.

The room was large and immaculate, with one side open to the view of the hills, and beyond it to the distant city. Behind the rows of shining, light brown desks sat the children, countless numbers of them, all dressed in white and navy uniform, all very quiet, looking at the teacher with serious black eyes.

How different this is from the Foreigners' Section, I thought, sitting down in the back row with Mother. "This spacious, well-lighted room, this building of steel, glass, imitation marble and polished woodwork — so beautiful, and so impersonal..."

A middle-aged lady in a dark-colored kimono stood on the platform holding a bamboo stick. Behind her a large map of Japan hung on the wall. "And now," she said, turning toward the blackboard and indicating a corner of the map with her stick, "who can tell me the name of this plain?"

"Yes, yes, yes, yes..." Abruptly the silence was broken; the room became filled with clamoring voices and hands raised, wavering, frantic, to catch the teacher's attention.

"Well then, all of you may tell me," said the teacher smiling.

The hands went fluttering down, and "Kanto Plain!" chorused the children at the top of their voices. The windowpanes shook with vibration, and the ancient clay figurine on the shelf trembled.

In silent wonder I stared at the rows of uniformed children, their eyes eager and bright under the straight black hair. Am I going to be one of them? But how? Somehow the thought was frightening. And sitting there among the host of children who were to be my classmates, my friends, I felt alien, and alone.

The first bell rang at five to eight. Hurry, hurry, get into the line before the roll call begins. Quick, hang your coat and hat in the locker, dash into the classroom and throw your satchel on your desk, then run down the corridor out to the courtyard — the girls are all there, lining up according to their height, one class after another. Hurry, hurry — I scurry through the lines and slip into my place, breathless. On the stone step, under the huge white crest of the Sacred Heart stands Madame Hirata, solemn and dignified. A breeze ruffles a strand of hair from her gray chignon. It's another glorious autumn day — the oak tree near Our Lady's grotto shines in the morning sun; the sky is deep blue, with bits of fleecy clouds like a new floss-silk coverlet... "There — that child in the third row, don't stand gaping up at the sky. Attention, please," says Madame Hirata. A quiet snicker spreads like a water ring among the girls. How strangely the new one behaves — she is, you know, a little different...

Another bell rings, and "Silence, children" from Madame Hirata. Motionless and rigid we stand, hands on our sides. Then all at once we turn around, facing toward the Imperial Palace. One — two — three — four — five — six, our heads go down in a deep bow, slowly, reverently. Hush, we are paying homage to the Emperor, the Father of all our fathers... Our heads come up with another count of six. Madame Hirata, still solemn, gives a final nod and disappears, and one by one the classes begin to move, walking in measured steps back to their classrooms, silent, unsmiling procession of blue and white uniforms...

Fifty minutes of class — dull, slow, and monotonous. Why does the teacher repeat so many times — the same thing over and over again? Why does it take so long to learn anything at all? "Teacher, Miss Hatsumi is drawing a picture in her notebook..." "Why do you look out of the window all the time, Miss Hatsumi? Aren't you interested in learning anything? One would think you were permitted such behavior in the Foreigners' Section..." Oh, but it was so different in the Foreigners' Section, I think to myself. So different — how, I cannot explain, but anyway different...

Ten minutes of recess in between classes — but you have to go up and play ball games on the roof. You aren't supposed to stay in classrooms. What — you want to stay and read, alone, all by yourself? But such things are simply not done. You must obey the rules. Why, no one dreams of doing otherwise.

How long — how long before the day is over, and three o'clock bell rings? I look at my wrist watch. "It isn't a good idea, to permit children to bring watches to school," remarks one of the teachers. "*Some* do nothing but look at their watches..."

Eight in the morning till half past three — five days a week, plus four hours on Saturday, herded from one place to another like an eager flock of sheep. "Your duty is to be a part of the whole. Your duty is to be a good Japanese..."

Why couldn't I absorb that all-important and intangible thing called the Right Japanese Spirit, when everyone else did, without, apparently any difficulty at all? In the Foreigners' Section it had been the Sacred Heart spirit — "Always be polite and courteous, children, don't run in the corridors and don't bang the door. Always be nice and kind to your inferiors and volunteer for the work you don't like." That was easy to understand, if not easy to do. But now, the Sacred Heart spirit and the Right Japanese Spirit were not altogether the same thing. As a matter of fact they seemed to be in direct conflict with each other at times...

To take one example, in the Japanese School it was perfectly permissible for the girls to blush and giggle instead of answering the teachers. In the Foreigners' Section such behavior would have been considered both uncourteous and idiotic. Another, and more important difference, however, concerned itself with one's attitude toward asking questions. In the Foreigners' Section you could have said, for instance, "I don't want to play *cache-cache* today, Mother. Why must we play *cache-cache* at all?" Or asked, "How many undergarments do you wear, Mother?" You might have to play *cache-cache* for the love of God, and Mother Welman might not speak to you for a whole week, but still you weren't punished for asking questions — provided you asked them politely enough.

But things weren't quite that simple in the Japanese School, and Mrs. Tsushima, our class mistress, was the first to recognize my lack of proper attitude. Mrs. Tsushima was a small, gentle person with a mild temperament and no sense of humor — perhaps that was the trouble. At any rate one morning — it was raining, a slight, late-autumn drizzle, silky, soft, incessant rain from the overhanging sky — I was hurrying on my way to the roll call when someone called me. I stopped, turned around, and saw the unsmiling face of Mrs. Tsushima approaching.

"You know, it's against the rule to wear sweaters at the morning ceremony," she said, coming up to me.

"But it's so cold," I said, glancing out of the window at the rain-drenched courtyard.

"A rule is a rule," said Mrs. Tsushima sternly. "Besides, you should wear a pullover and not a cardigan. It's also a regulation."

I looked down at my navy sweater with a *croisé* pattern, light, soft and warm. "But why," I protested. "Mother told me to wear this because it's so cold today..."

"Don't talk back," said Mrs. Tsushima, flushing. "You are always saying 'But why'..."

"But..."

"There you are again! Didn't they teach you manners in the Foreigners' Section at all? You'll never be a good Japanese the way you behave..."

Why was it being a good Japanese to stand in the drizzle without a sweater or a coat? I wondered, going back to the locker with my discarded cardigan. Even if it was a matter of ten minutes, it still sounded a little unreasonable — especially when I caught colds so quickly.

That incident, although trivial in itself, somehow marked the beginning of a procession of troubles. Everything I did and said became wrong. I wasn't eager enough about anything. I was disobedient, I was forgetful, I questioned authority. And always at the end, "You lack the right spirit..."

Before I knew, I had become the problem child of the school. And Mother received a polite invitation to "Talk things over" with Madame Hirata.

"What is the trouble with you, Reiko?" asked Mother with a sigh when she came home from the conference. "What do you *do* at school?"

"Nothing, Mother," I answered, nonplused.

"Madame Hirata said you were *unmanageable*— don't you ever listen to your teachers?"

"I do, Mother," I said guardedly. They talked so much, you couldn't really help hearing them from time to time...

"Do you do what they tell you to do?"

"I suppose so, Mother—I do what other children do." There really wasn't any choice in the matter, I added to myself silently.

"Then what *don't* you do?" asked Mother helplessly.

"Perhaps it's what she *says* rather than what she *does*," suggested my youngest sister who was going to the middle school. "Our ethics teacher said Reiko refused to read the lessons with the rest of the class, because she said forty-six children reading in chorus made her head ache."

I looked down in silence. Really, if that tattletale girl next to me didn't raise her hand and tell the teacher I wasn't reading—I was moving my mouth at least.

"Then she asked the history teacher whether it's patriotic to say everything Japanese is good," continued my sister resentfully. "I get to be the whipping girl, Reiko. And everybody thinks you are a little queer..."

"The gymnastic teacher told me Reiko is totally uncooperative," said Mother.

"But Mother, I feel so silly jumping up and down in the gym, wearing bloomers. I hate bloomers, Mother. And I don't see why they have anything to do with being patriotic..."

"What about the games — don't you like them at all?" asked Mother hopefully.

"No — not very much," I answered, closing my eyes with a shudder. "Some of them are awfully mean, Mother — chasing one another, trying to hit a girl with a ball, and it really hurts when you get hit..."

"Well, I don't see why you can't behave the way all the others do," said Mother wearily.

"But Mother," I said, looking up at her, puzzled. "Why must I behave like everyone else, when I don't want to, and when I can't understand why?"

Mother looked at me and sighed. "It was a mistake, wasn't it?" she said to herself. "It was a mistake sending you to the Foreigners' Section..."

Once my reputation was established, it persisted. Teachers looked at me, shook their heads, and sighed. One complained she didn't like the way I said "Yes, teacher." There was, she claimed, a ring of insolence and defiance, a tone of condescending mockery in my "Yes, teacher." In almost every class my behavior was criticized and condemned. And I suffered, for although I had the good will to conform, I didn't know how.

"Why don't they tell me what to do?" I asked Mother once, "instead of just saying everything I do is bad...I don't know how to behave anymore."

Again and again reports were sent to my mother, much to her annoyance. What could she do — what did the teachers suggest she do about me? To change school was unthinkable. Why, what would Reverend Mother say? Going back to the Foreigners' Section was out of the question. It would only complicate things between the lay faculty of the Japanese School and the veiled faculty of the Foreigners' Section. Besides, Reiko is so westernized already, one would be afraid to think of further results at an English school...

I wish somebody had told me then that it was neither my fault nor that of my teachers. That it was Japan that was changing — from a decade of liberalism to a totalitarian militarism and controlled thought...While I was growing, statesmen were being assassinated by a group of army officers, and all branches of government became annexed to the Ministry of War. That the "right Japanese spirit" meant simply frowning on anything foreign, and it was for the nation a time not of speculation but of unquestioning obedience. But those things cannot be told to a nine-year-old and understood...

Actually, I think Mother sympathized with me, although she never said so. Once she remarked when she thought I was out of hearing, "Things weren't quite that way when I was young — it must be the change of times...I don't particularly care for these *modern* educational methods." But since everyone else's children were going through with it, why couldn't Reiko? So I went on as before, blindly groping for the Right Spirit, stumbling at every dangerous corner, creating more and more trouble, and looking forward to each holiday as a day of redemption.

Sometimes I look back, and ask myself, "Was I that bad — really *that* bad?" Perhaps I was. I don't deny that I was unenthusiastic and uncooperative, that I asked questions which probably should never have been asked. But if I was bad, I paid the penalty too. I lost sleep, became pale, nervous, touchy, and jumped like a rabbit at every mention of my name...

"Why, the child is just skin and bones," exclaimed one of Father's friends. "Are you sure she isn't suffering from child tuberculosis?"

"I don't know," said Mother sadly. "She's never been too strong. Perhaps the school is a little too much strain on her."

"Whatever it may be, you had better take her to a doctor," advised Father's friend.

"Perhaps I should," agreed Mother doubtfully.

I hoped she would forget about the suggestion, for I never liked medical examinations. But one day the following week Mother took me to the Keio Hospital. During what seemed like a long, long time I was X-rayed, tapped at, and questioned, while one doctor after another came in, stroked my hair, clicked his tongue, squinted and shook his head. Then all of them went into a conference in the next room. We sat there and waited till one doctor, the oldest of the group, came and called Mother in. Through the closed door I heard whispers and coughs, and Mother exclaiming, "But that's impossible — she is only nine years old!" Then someone said something and they all laughed.

After a few minutes Mother came out with a vaguely puzzled expression on her face, and we left the hospital.

On the way home Mother told me I was suffering from a nervous breakdown. "Oh," I said unimpressed. I could have been mentally deranged for all I cared. The only thing that depressed me was the thought of more doctors' visits, pills, diets and injections — all of which were just an added misery to my none too happy existence.

"You might have to stop school for a while, Reiko," continued Mother.

I looked up, surprised. "Really, Mother?" I began eagerly, then checked myself. If I sounded too cheerful Mother might change her mind... "For how long?" I asked, trying my best to look pale and indifferent.

"I don't know yet — perhaps for a half a year or so. But we must wait and see."

I relapsed into silence, and looked out of the car window. Everything — the busy streets, dusty trees drooping over the sidewalk, running, crying children, little shops with oblong cotton flags, women with babies tied to their backs — everything looked brighter, more interesting. And for the first time in nearly six months, I felt almost happy.

Being a problem child had its compensations.

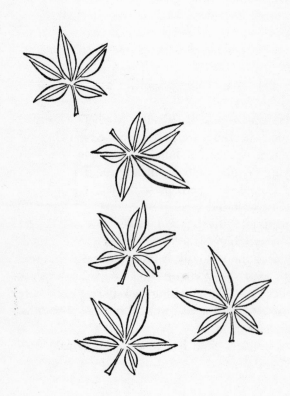

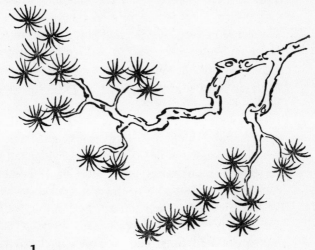

Udumbara

Etsu said she felt lonesome in our house near the sea. She said it was too quiet. But I didn't mind it at all. On the contrary, I thought Kamakura was much better with the noisy summer crowd gone. Now the little resort town slumbered, with the spring dust settling on its empty white streets, and houses closed for the year stood behind the high walls, under the sandy pine trees, silent and deserted.

Even the sea drowsed under the warm spring sun, mild-blue and tranquil, lapping lazily on the curving white shores. Silvery vapor danced on the gleaming, copper-colored seaweed, and the fishermen's nets, limp, dark brown, sprawled silently on the vacant beach, beside the sap-green hills sloping gently down to the sea. Not a soul there was — except perhaps for a fishing boat or two, rocking far away on the turquoise-blue water, or tiny, ethereal footprints of the plovers on the glistening black sand.

We didn't do much those days — Etsu and I. But I didn't mind. Walks in the morning, and after lunch reading, taking naps, or sitting in the corridor and watching the plum blossoms open little by little near the slanting eaves, listening to the soft, melodious voice of the bush warbler — then toward the evening seeing the sun go down in the dappled sky, away beyond the densely wooded hills, and rose-colored clouds turning amethyst, then fading into darkness.

"Little Mistress isn't bored? Little Mistress is not lonesome?"

Poor Etsu — no matter what I said, I couldn't convince her. I couldn't convince her that I enjoyed doing nothing. That I enjoyed being alone.

"No, I'm not lonesome, Etsu. Come here, I'll read to you."

Etsu sat there, beside my silk sitting cushion, on the matted floor, her slight oval face bent over a piece of sewing, listening politely as I read anything, everything out loud to her. Old Japanese legends, medieval tales of war and adventure, English children's stories — she listened to them all without protest, even, I remember, when I went through the whole of *Water Babies,* and I doubt whether she understood a word.

At night, the silence became oppressive. You could hear it hanging over the roof, enveloping the house in darkness, filtering in through the sliding doors and pressing on the eardrums, like a huge, resounding, prolonged echo.

"I think I'll go to bed, Etsu. It's getting late."

"Very well, Reiko Sama." Did she sound slightly relieved then, always? And every night, before she turned off the little paper-framed lamp beside my pillow, she would say, "Tomorrow perhaps we shall go to the Hachiman Shrine for the annual feast there. Tomorrow perhaps I can think of something amusing to do."

Good, faithful, worrying Etsu — didn't she know that I wasn't particularly interested in going anywhere? That to me, one shrine was more or less the same as another?

The same thing with Mother. Every week, when she came to visit me, we went somewhere. A stroll to the famed Hachiman Shrine, with its ninety-nine steps of stone and the giant maidenhair tree, and the red lacquered *no* stage, and the sprawling lotus pond under the wisteria-hung pergola. We climbed the ninety-nine steps of stone and scattered soya beans to the fluttering doves, and threw wheat cakes to the huge crimson carp in the pond. Or we took a shiny black horse-drawn carriage to the distant cape, and dined at tea houses overlooking the sea.

And always, "Why aren't you eating, Reiko? Don't you like this wreath-shell roast? It is very good — the house is known for this dish..."

"I'm not very hungry, Mother."

"But you should eat something...Etsu said your appetite is very poor. Perhaps I should bring something novel from Tokyo..."

She did bring something novel all the time — bean cakes, pickles, sweets from famed pastry shops, and if not eatables, a new doll, a dress, books and toys, and once a set of lapis lazuli marbles — opaque, misty blue stones they were, shining golden azure when held against the sun. Anything to distract the child's mind — Etsu says you brood too much. . .

"But I don't brood, Mother."

"Then what do you do all day?"

"Nothing, Mother."

"That's what I mean, Reiko. You should do something to amuse yourself. Why don't you play with your cousins — you used to, last summer. Remember?"

But last summer was long since gone, and now all my cousins were busy at school. No more fishing trips and sailboating, no more cicada-hunting among the woods...

Gradually I began evading Etsu, her ever watchful eyes, and going for a walk all by myself. Not far, however. For Etsu would have been scolded if I had. Only very rarely, when Kei Chan, my youngest cousin, came to play with me, was I allowed to go out for a whole afternoon. And it was one of those long walks with Kei Chan that I met my friend, who lived in a temple on the side of a hill.

One day we were on our way home from the sea, having spent hours watching hermit crabs scurry in and out of the clear, limpid pools of water between the rocks. It was late afternoon, and we were walking, hand in hand, in the soft, yellow sunshine, feeling a little tired. But then I didn't want to go home — not quite yet. So when we passed the gate of Myohonji, an old temple not far from my house, I remembered we used to go there quite often the summer before.

"I wonder what happened to the snake in the pond, Kei Chan. Do you think he's still there?"

"I don't think so. He's gone to sleep somewhere."

"Where?"

"Oh, I don't know — somewhere in the mountainside. He won't come out till June."

"Let's go and see anyway, Kei Chan."

"If you want to," said Kei Chan reluctantly. "But there isn't anything to see now..."

"It doesn't matter, Kei Chan. I don't want to go home yet..."

"We shouldn't stay too long, though. Etsu said your mother is coming from Tokyo, with a doctor."

"I know," I said, pulling at his hand.

So we went through the wooden temple gate, and up between rows of giant *passanias*. The air was damp, crystal cool under the shadow of the trees, and sunshine, sifting through the leaves, rippled on the moist, stone-speckled ground. It was very quiet — only the rustle of the leaves, and water dripping somewhere.

We walked up the narrow slippery stairs and stopped under the inner temple gate, between two faded Deva gods, sitting forgotten under the eaves. In front of us, on the empty, sunny square, fell the shadow of the temple building, and next to it behind a low fence stood a large *kaido* tree, heavily laden with bright coral flowers, burning in the glow of the sinking sun.

"We should go, Reiko Chan," repeated my cousin hesitantly. "Your mother will be angry if we don't. . ."

I didn't answer, but began walking toward the *kaido* tree. "Come on," I said coaxingly. "I want to see if the little red crabs are still there in the moat. You used to catch them for me last summer — remember?"

Kei Chan stood under the carved frieze of the temple gate, hands in his pockets, frowning.

"If *you* want to go home, why don't you?" I said, losing patience.

For a while my cousin kept on standing, his lips pressed together, as if wondering what to do. Then abruptly he turned around, and went running down the stairs, whistling.

All alone, I walked past the flowering *kaido* tree, and then to the edge of the waterless moat. But there weren't any crabs in the grass-covered bottom, or on the rough stone facing that looked damp and cold. There wasn't anything living, except a day-fly hovering over the round wooden railing of the temple corridor, and beneath the cracked gallery floor some scattered dandelions. Even the pond water looked dead, and under its mud-green surface half-rotten weeds floated lifelessly.

Across the moat, against the mountainside, stood old graves, the lettering on the tombstones almost erased by wind and rain. What were those people like? I wondered idly. Some of their names were still famous in history books. But five hundred years is a very long time — and nothing remained of them but a bunch of mossy stones. No more scarlet armor and brocaded robes...

I turned away from the temple and walked down the little path beneath the round pagoda tree, not knowing quite where I wanted to go. Then I saw someone through the pine groves, crouching on a piece of clearing a little further down. I stared again, and saw that it was a bonze, picking grass and throwing it into a basket beside him on the ground. As I walked up to him, the sound of my wooden sandals fell softly on the moss-covered stones. But the bonze did not look up. And for a while I stood there beside him, watching without a word.

Finally I broke the silence. "What are you doing?" I asked.

"Weeding," said the bonze, and became silent again. He was a slender old man, clad in a black rough-woven robe, with a shaved scalp that looked like a taro corm.

After a while I decided to help him. So, gathering the hem of my kimono in one hand, I bent down to pull stray bits of grass from the ground. The air was still, and a shadow of a pine tree fell between us, dark and unmoving. High above, a black kite circled, sinister and graceful, gliding through the air.

Finally my knees began to ache, so I stood up. The bonze raised his taro-corm head and looked at me. His face was lean, bronzed, with deep fine lines around his eyes, running down his cheeks. Surprisingly delicate it was, like an ancient *no* mask. But his keen black eyes looked quiet and kindly, almost humorous.

"Thank you for your trouble," said he, faintly smiling.

I smiled back. I felt shy, but then I wanted to say something.

"Do you live here?" I asked.

The bonze nodded, pointing toward a shingled roof half hidden among the cassia trees, further down the hill.

"Do you live alone?"

"No," said the bonze. "There are many others — both young and old."

"What do you do?"

"What do we do?" said the bonze, standing up. "Well, that is a hard thing to say ... Reading Sutras would be about it, I suppose."

"And what else?"

"Nothing in particular."

"Don't you have to study at all?"

"Ha, ha," laughed the bonze, slapping mud off his hands and knees. "We don't study — not, at least, in the sense that you might. We paint pictures though, at times."

"Is that all?"

"Then we sit down and meditate."

"On what?"

"On nothing."

"Oh," I said, and fell silent. It must be difficult to think about nothing, I thought to myself.

The thin, cranelike priest stretched his back, and

shielding his eyes with one hand gazed down toward the city that slept under the lilac-colored haze. "Fine weather," he murmured. "Farmers will be happy..." Then turning to me he asked, "Have you come to look at the *kaido* tree?"

"No — not particularly," I said. "But it is very beautiful..."

"Quite, quite," said the bonze, gathering up his basket. "It is a very old tree. It has been there since long before we were born, and it will be there long after we are gone. Well, I must be returning now..."

Just then Etsu came up the stairs, looking flushed and worried. She stopped under the faded gold tablet hung on the temple gate and gazed around restlessly. Then she saw me standing in the clearing near the pine grove.

"Oh, there you are, Reiko Sama," she said, her voice full of mild reproach. "I have looked all over for you — the Mistress has arrived and is waiting for your return..."

Reluctantly I turned to go. The thin little priest looked at me again, a flickering smile in his deeply sunken eyes. "Come back sometime," he said, then with small toddling steps, but with a curious, remote dignity, he went down the slope and disappeared.

Much later I came to know that he was the chief priest of Myohonji, the ancient and much honored temple near my home. But I had no notion about it then. Really, it was a bit difficult to imagine him as a high-ranking priest, revered by all for his knowledge and wisdom — when I saw him sauntering in the garden, a pair of scissors in one hand, a bunch of wild flowers in the other. Sometimes I met him, probably on his way to a Buddhist service at a parishioner's home, walking down the hill with small steps, leaning on a slender, crooked cane and looking like a faded jonquil in his yellow hood.

Sometimes I had a cup of tea in his study — a tiny little room at the edge of the rectory, overlooking the city and beyond it to the distant sea. It was very quiet, and always, a faint smell of sandalwood clung in the shadowy air. An aged gold altar stood in the corner of the room, and next to it, on the leaden-colored wall of the alcove, hung a picture of Dharma. Easygoing and jolly he seemed, hands clasped on his fat abdomen, a meditative smile on his cheeks.

We never talked much, the old priest and I. And when we did, it was of little things, small things around us — of weather and the fading peonies, of the new green leaves on the *chinensis* tree in the garden ... Very rarely did he mention anything about his religion, and even then his words sounded vague, cryptic, full of meaning ...

"Look at the white flower under the hedge," said he once. "That is Udumbara — the flower of paradise."

"Is there such a thing as paradise?" I asked, very skeptically.

The old bonze smiled. "If you think there is, there is," said he. "If you think there isn't, there isn't."

"Then what about Hades," I asked. "And Yama with his tongue-plucker and the sizzling oil pot ..."

"That is the same. If you think there is ..."

There was no end to it. I never knew what he really thought about anything. But still I liked to visit the old priest, and to sit on the rush-matted floor under the dark transom windows with a teacup in my hands, listening to the murmur of the iron kettle on the square sunken hearth. There was something very peaceful about it all.

April and May went by swiftly, and one day Mother told me I had to go back to school.

"So soon, Mother?"

"Yes, Reiko. You don't want to fail one year, do you? You should go back at least for the term examinations..."

School again. How many years till I graduate? I wondered hopelessly. Eight years — eight long years stretched in front of me, endless, menacing. And once again I felt listless, unhappy, apprehensive, while day after day went by, each one more precious than another, like lingering bits of treasure dwindling swiftly, relentlessly.

The day before I left Kamakura I went to say goodbye to the old priest. He was sitting in the corridor of his room, painting. And as I walked around the thicket to the front garden, the bonze looked up with a brush in his hand.

"Well, well," he said. "I haven't seen you for a while. Sit down here — the picture is almost finished."

I sat down on the edge of the corridor, and looked down toward the city. Among the deep green foliage, the distant roofs shone cold and silver. And above, in the clouded sky, white herons fluttered past, crying.

"There," said the priest, holding up the piece of Chinese paper. "This is for a parishioner — he wouldn't listen till I promised..."

I looked at the picture. A bottle gourd, a twisted vine, a couple of leaves and his name, that was all.

"Now shall we have a cup of tea?" said the bonze, turning toward the sunken hearth and reaching out for the iron kettle.

"I can't stay very long," I said. "I came to say goodbye."

"Oh?" said the bonze. "Are you going away?"

"I have to go home — back to school." My voice must have sounded troubled, a bit forlorn. The priest took up the kettle, poured out two cups of tea, then looked at me gently, pushing over one of the cups. "You don't like school?" he asked.

"No."

"That is strange," said the bonze meditatively. "A person your age must like to be with young people..."

I shook my head, unable to explain. Above us, the white herons kept on passing. The air became damp, cool, shadowy. The thin little priest looked up toward the sky. "Rain," he murmured. "It will be raining before long..."

In silence I held the teacup in my hands and took a sip. The pale green tea was warm, and smelled faintly of citron flowers. "I wish," I said, "I could live somewhere like this, and not go to school."

The old priest smiled. "Isn't that a little too early at your age?" he said. "There are other things you must want to do."

"Not particularly," I said dismally, putting down the teacup. "But I suppose it can't be helped — there are things that can't be helped."

"Perhaps so," said the bonze, then added to himself, "But still, things are what you make them to be — people create hell in their minds, and so can they create heaven..." Sitting there, hands folded under his black robe, he looked like a carved wooden statue, remote, detached, forgetting that I was there...

Going out of the paneled garden door, I noticed a cluster of firefly grass underneath the hedge, tiny, blue, and delicate. But there was something missing — the white udumbara flower was gone. Where did it go? I wondered whimsically. Perhaps it went back to paradise... Somebody's paradise, if not the old bonze's. For I didn't believe he thought there was one, really.

Then I remembered — I don't know why — the words he told me long time ago. "Look at the flower of Udumbara — it looks whiter under the rain. Look at the pine trees — wind may blow, but they are not concerned..."

I shrugged my shoulders, and went running down the stone steps, between the rows of aged *passanias*, tall, straight, reaching toward the sky — wondering.

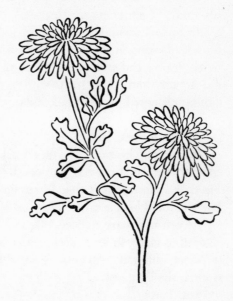

Epilogue

THE DAY I left my country, I went to say goodbye
to my father. It wasn't that we lived in different houses,
but as the years went by, we children had grown pro-
gressively apart from him. Now we seldom dined
together, and it was rarely that he saw me. For, as my
brothers and sisters got married and left our home one
by one, Father became more and more absorbed in his
philosophical writing, spending his days in the isolated
study, with only the stacks of manuscripts and the
perpetual rustle of his pen.

So I went to say goodbye to him.

"Father," I said, kneeling down on the threshold of his study, "I am going to America."

He turned around and took off his glasses. "Well," he said, looking at me as if I were some strange object newly introduced to his life. I felt uneasy, as I always did around him. The room was very quiet. Outside, cicadas clamored on the paulownia.

"What time are you leaving?" he finally asked.

"At five o'clock, Father."

"Is that so," he said. He didn't ask me when I was coming back, or for what purpose I was going abroad. He took it for granted that I was going to study. He knew I would be home when my studies were over.

"As you may have noticed," he said slowly, carefully, "I tried to give you an education that would enable you to meet different situations — in different kinds of worlds, shall we say..."

"Yes, Father."

"I don't know whether it was any use — but you will find that out for yourself."

"Yes, Father."

He became silent again, and I wondered whether I should leave. "Well," I began, but he stopped me.

"Just a minute," said Father, turning toward a lacquered fancy chest that stood near his desk. He opened a drawer and took out a small object in a brocaded bag.

"This is a sword that belonged to your grandmother," said Father, unlacing the cords of faded twill silk.

"But Father, I thought you gave it to my sister when she was married..."

"Your mother thought it was not necessary, be-sides..." He paused. The sword was a very old one, with ivory-studded hilt and a guard of engraved silver. What am I going to do with it? I wondered.

"I trust that you will not do anything to defile the name of our ancestors," said Father, giving me the sword.

"No, Father."

"Your mother is a little too modern. She thinks I place importance on outdated things."

"Yes, Father."

"All right." He turned around and gazed at his open book. "Please go," he said without looking at me. "Study hard."

Different situations in different kinds of worlds, I thought, walking down the long corridor that con-nected Father's study to the main wing of our house. Haven't I already met enough situations that were baffling? To my father belonged the life of quiet con-templation and aestheticism. But the world in which I grew up was one of overflowing Western civilization— an era when the remnants of our tradition were rapidly disappearing in a medley of imported cultures.

Where do we go from here? I wondered, looking at the polished wooden corridor and at the long, low eaves slanting over the lawn.

"Come in for a minute," said Mother from her living room. "I was looking around for some trinkets, but there aren't very many left..."

Mother's trinkets turned out to be a large piece of uncut jade, several alexandrites, a zircon and an opal ring.

"But you won't have anything left," I protested.

"I don't want anything," said Mother. "I'd give you a lot more if I could..." The bulk of her jewelry was given up during the war — what Mother didn't give to my sisters when they got married.

"You have a set of pearls," said Mother, "so I'm not worried about that. But really, you have so little of anything else..."

"It doesn't matter, Mother. If I had them, I might lose them anyway." When I said those words, I remembered suddenly, a scene from long ago. Same kind of morning. In the same room. Was it spring? I didn't remember any more...

"Reiko Chan," Mother calls me softly. I look up. On the matted floor are boxes of pearls, a carved white jade pendant and green jade brooches, agate sashbands and a diamond ring. "May I have one?" "Yes." I pick up the diamond ring. Mother smiles. "You'll have to wait for that," she says. "Someday, when you get married..." There is a stray pearl shining in the warm sun, and a small lady's watch — a kind that is called "a sleeve watch." Gold, heavy and delicately wrought, with a heart-shaped medal attached to it by a chain. "You may have that," says Mother, "if you promise not to lose it..."

"I still have your gold watch, Mother," I said.

Mother looked up with a puzzled expression on her face. "Watch? What watch?"

"Your sleeve watch, Mother, with the golden heart."

"Oh yes," said Mother smiling. "You still do? It was

a long time ago, wasn't it?" She looked down reminiscently at the box of trinkets. There were streaks of white in her hair.

"I wonder," she said after a pause, "whether I shall be alive when you come back."

"Oh Mother..." I hated to hear her talk that way. I knew she was thinking about a million little worries—war and the property tax and the rising cost of living. Mother always became pessimistic when she remembered those things.

"Oh well," she said quite cheerfully, recovering herself. "So long as I know that you will be all right..."

"I will be all right, Mother. After all, I'm not a child any more."

"Well, I suppose that's true," said Mother, then added, suddenly serious, "Remember—that no matter what happens, this will always be your home."

"I know, Mother." I may have sounded short, but then I was thinking—a thought that I didn't really know how to tell her. I shall always come back, I said to myself, and you will always be here. For *you* are my home, and my country, which I love—both you and Father.